The Solar Triangle

A. G. Hayes

Savant Books and Publications
Honolulu, HI, USA
2017

Published in the USA by Savant Books and Publications
2630 Kapiolani Blvd #1601
Honolulu, HI 96826
http://www.savantbooksandpublications.com

Printed in the USA

Edited by Kaethe Kauffman
Cover by Daniel S. Janik

13 digit ISBN: 9780997247244

Dedication

To Lea

The story you're about to read never happened. However, it could have, and may yet.

- A. G. Hayes

Chapter 1

Waves smashed against the one square mile of jagged black rock that comprised the home of Flangenan Lighthouse. The lighthouse had clung tenaciously to the rocky outcroppings three miles west of the Isle of Tiree for over two hundred years.

Flangenan Lighthouse, to a sea-going navigator, was a mere speck in the Atlantic. A place of solitude where even the screech of sea gulls no longer sounded, as if they too had been switched off with the beacons that had once flashed their warning across the turbulent sea.

"We chose it for its neutrality. The Brits opted for its inaccessibility and the Israelis chose it for its impregnability." Agent Joe Falk's low voice crackled into the earphones of Agent Susan Koski, seated beside him, blond and petite, but alert as she swept her binoculars across the vastness of the dark green sea below. Falk brushed a hank of chestnut hair out of his eyes as he swung the helicopter in a tight circle above the craggy island. "The Allies used the island in World War II as a lookout for German shipping movements. It's been abandoned ever since. The lighthouse was decommissioned in the fifties, and, as we know today, ships plying the rigors of the North Atlantic use GPS satellite," Falk explained.

Flangenan Lighthouse was soon to be inhabited once again, this time, by those who knew little of life in a cylindrical tower amidst a sea of many moods. Koski's ponytail bobbed as she turned her head and focused her binoculars on the lighthouse. Once crisp and white, now in the wintry morning sun, its conical structure embedded into the northernmost tip of the land was weather-worn to a splotchy grey. She scrutinized a concrete bunker added to the west curve of the lighthouse and another built into the east face of the rock cliff.

The helicopter circled one more time around the lighthouse and then set course back to Tiree. Although the weather was bright and clear for November, nonetheless it could change in a moment. Falk leaned forward, watching the cliffs of Tiree flash beneath them. The three-mile distance seemed to take no time since they had left the lighthouse.

The copter approached a grass landing strip marked with a red and white radial, then, with a classic nose-up angle, lowered gently to earth. Falk shut down the engine and unsnapped his seat belt. The slowing whoosh of the blades cut through the cold Scottish air, wound down and stopped while Falk and Koski eased out of the machine. A brightly painted logo on the side of the aircraft depicting two sea birds in flight against a yellow and orange sun reflected a splash of color as a shaft of watery sunlight momentarily peeped from behind a low bank of fast moving storm clouds being swept in from the sea.

"Made it back just in time," Falk grunted, scanning the sky. "They warned me how quick weather changes up here at this time of the year." He referred to the contacts he had met in the coastal town of Oban, on the Scottish mainland two days before.

"Scotland in November—this could be a wet and windy assignment, Joe." Koski tugged up the collar of her thick down jacket as she shrugged her shoulders and thrust her hands deep into the large patch pockets. A seasoned agent, she had worked in far worse conditions than this.

This was their fifth assignment together. They'd first met in Nevada when Falk was assigned to lead a task force to solve the mysterious serial killings of lawyers in California and Nevada.

Falk remembered that first meeting. They'd both suffered personal losses. Koski had a husband who was accused of selling drugs while a member of the Las Vegas police department; he was now an ex-husband serving time in the Nevada State Prison in Carson City.

Falk's wife had died in a freak accident several months earlier. The loss affected him more than he realized. Sadness mixed with the gnawing guilt of not being able to get to her to help her before she died had haunted him with a frustrated sense of helplessness.

Over the years, the situation between Koski and Falk had changed. Now, they were more than just a team.

Falk nodded to a man in a faded orange boiler suit that trotted over to tie down the helicopter. To him, Falk and Koski probably seemed like two members of yet another group of do-gooders. Stopping besides the copter, the mechanic looked at the logo and read, *The foxes have holes and the birds of the air have nests.*

"Takes all kinds," he muttered to himself as he went about the job of securing the aircraft. "As long as they pay, whatever they do is fine with me. I'll sell them all the fuel they want. This time of the year, there's hardly any helicopters around."

Switching on the ignition of a rented SUV, Falk put it in drive and bumped across the grass field toward a five-barred gate that served as an entrance to the small airstrip. He headed out onto a narrow two-lane road.

The four-mile return journey to the hotel proved uneventful. Now, cleaned up and rested, Koski and Falk relaxed on a well-worn leather couch in the lounge of the old Glenn Morgan Hotel on the Hebridean Isle of Tiree, staring unblinkingly at a cold, blustery day that rattled the window frames and dashed icy rain into rivulets across the panes of glass. It was their second day at the Glenn Morgan.

Koski sighed. "What a place: twelve miles long and six miles at its widest point, covering an area of thirty square miles of total boredom. Why would Stewart want to base us here?"

"This time of the year, there's not many visitors and little chance of the media getting curious. As far as the locals know, we're part of an ornithologists' team researching sea birds of the North Atlantic."

"How are the others getting here?" Koski asked.

"Jack Tanner and Doctor Kevin Clayton are flying in on Highlands and Islands Air," Falk said. "They'll land at the Tyree airstrip and take a car to the hotel. Commander Harris and Professor Victor Teesdale will be crossing over from Oban on the ferry. Doctor Jacob Jenner and Ms. Courtney Spencer will arrive by private plane."

Koski grunted. "A small plane in this weather?"

"Courtney Spencer is piloting the private plane in from Glasgow. I hear she's good."

"She better be." A gust of wind again rattled the hotel windows.

"I suppose this is the last place anyone would expect to find three world class scientists specializing in renewable energy and solar chemistry." Leaning back, he laced his fingers behind his head, ruffling his rich, dark-brown hair.

Koski nodded.

"The security at the lighthouse must be awesome," Falk chuckled. "Especially when you consider that the security on this island is in the hands of only one constable."

"You have to be kidding."

"Nope."

"And out at the lighthouse?"

"The scientists will have their own security people."

Koski was silent. The name Tanner rang a bell, but she could not remember why. "Do we know this guy, Jack Tanner?"

"No. But maybe you read about him a couple of years ago. He was in charge of an abortive attempt to flush out a commune, a home-style militia in Idaho. A couple of kids were killed. He took the blame and bad press."

Koski nodded. "I remember something about that. Now he's in charge of this operation? That's just great," Koski said, rolling her blue-gray eyes upward.

"There's an old saying, Koski, that politics makes for strange bedfellows."

Chapter 2

The fierce Negev desert sun blazed down on a bleached concrete runway in the middle of a hot, barren wasteland. Flat, decaying white buildings shimmered in the distance. Two Israeli soldiers stood beside Jacob Jenner, a brooding man in his late forties, his eyes magnified and obscured behind thick lenses. He glanced at his watch to remind himself of the time: 1440 hours. The plane was precisely on time. Flies buzzed annoyingly around the three men in the silent, acrid heat.

Jacob Jenner shaded his eyes and, hearing the drone of a small aircraft, looked up and watched as the private plane circled over the buildings and made its final approach to the runway, setting down with a squeak of tires and a puff of dust.

Jenner nodded to the two soldiers, picked up his suitcase, and headed to the plane that had taxied in close to them.

The cockpit door opened, and the pilot eased out and stood on the wing. Courtney Spencer was tall and slender.

Jenner could not see her face, as the sun blinded him. Standing with feet apart and hands on hips, she appeared like a modern day Sun God, a golden phoenix.

Then Courtney spoke, "Hello again, Doctor Jenner."

Jenner stopped and looked up, shading his eyes. "I didn't know we'd met."

"Two years ago at the Weizmann Institute." Courtney moved slightly and now he could see her face, pale and beautiful.

"Can't imagine how I'd forget."

Courtney reached down and shook his hand. "Your wife, she was still alive then. Welcome aboard. I'm from the Knesset."

Jenner nodded, handed up his suitcase, then went around to the passenger door and scrambled up onto the wing and into the cockpit. There was no further conversation as Courtney took the controls and throttled the plane down the runway into a smooth take off.

Glancing back, Jenner saw the two Israeli soldiers lift their heads as if watching until the plane was out of sight and silence returned to the desert. He turned, imagining them slowly sauntering back to their jeep.

Chapter 3

At the same time, Jack Tanner was sitting at his desk in Washington, D.C. listening to a voice on his intercom. "He'll cooperate. Just see he watches his manners and keeps his mind on the job. We all know how easily distracted he can get."

Lines of disillusion had set into a face no longer young. Tanner flicked a speck from his razor-cut Madison Avenue suit. "Yes, sir, I know."

The voice on the intercom continued: "Jack, this is essentially an American operation, so that puts you right up front where it shows. You need this one. Pull this off successfully and you're back on top. I guarantee."

Tanner cleared his throat softly. "Thank you, sir." He flicked the switch. Momentarily lost in thought, he rose, crossed over to a wall mirror and took a long, hard look at his reflection. His expression darkened. Then, twisting away, he crossed to a window and stared at the dome of the Capitol Building in the distance. "This time…whatever it takes. I guarantee." Turning to face the door, he picked up a suitcase and exited.

The Solar Triangle

Chapter 4

From a hotel on a narrow avenue housing a row of small, elite hotels, a middle-aged man emerged and waited under the canopy of The Nelson. Above his head the cloth thrashed and rapped in the wind and rain. Squat and barrel chested, he looked about him, scowled at the rain with disdain and shifted uncomfortably inside the thick tweeds. He was Commander Harold Harris, Royal Navy, Order of the British Empire, and now of the British Foreign Office.

A hotel door attendant hastened to the commander and covered him with an oversized umbrella, escorting him to a waiting Rolls Royce. The commander entered the rear of the car. The door closed and the doorman leaned forward with a salute. "Have a good trip, Commander."

Harris smiled. It gave him a deep sense of pleasure that everyone on the row knew him.

The Rolls moved off through the rain. Seated next to the commander was a tired looking aristocrat. "We've packed you warm clothes, Commander. Shocking weather where you're going." The Rolls continued its journey through torrential rain as a thunderstorm moved in overhead, blackening the sky.

Later that day, somewhere in rural England, the Rolls splashed along a country lane and came to a stop outside a whitewashed cottage. The chauffeur got out and dashed through the downpour to the front door of the small home.

In the rear of the Rolls, the commander and the aristocrat sat in silence, listening to the rain.

A few minutes later the chauffeur returned with a suitcase, loaded it in the trunk, and announced, "Hiz wife sez 'e won't be a minute."

The commander bridled. "Damn it! Where the devil is that man? We mustn't let the Americans get there first."

The chauffeur jerked his head toward a high privet hedge in front of the garden and grinned. The commander and the aristocrat leaned forward, curious.

From the other side of the hedge a head popped up, the face ancient and crinkled, the high forehead covered by a turn of the century Sou'wester style hat. Professor Victor Teesdale, rain pouring upon him, held up a seedling. "Early cropper. The dwarf variety with excellent flavor. But it needs protection from the rain, you see. Just have to be sure they're covered. Be right with you."

Commander Harris turned to the aristocrat. "Are you sure he's our best?"

Chapter 5

"The guy in the tweed suit," Koski nodded toward the bar. "I heard one of the staff call him 'Commander.' He arrived today with the eccentric looking man with the huge forehead, who's sitting next to him."

Falk saw the person Koski referred to as the commander, a blustery sort, obviously used to giving orders. He and the man she had described as eccentric were deep in conversation, sipping from large glasses that contained, no doubt, scotch. A full briefing for all of the scientists and security agents would be forthcoming upon the arrival of Jack Tanner of the U. S. State Department.

"I also talked to one of the housemaids this morning and she mentioned that last week this place was almost empty." Koski stopped talking as a shapely blonde and a studious-looking man wearing thick glasses entered. They paused in the doorway, scanned the room, then headed to a table next to a window overlooking the small harbor and sat down.

Falk checked his watch. "I'm sure you reinforced the fact that we are a couple of bird watchers."

Koski smiled and nodded. "Of course."

The Solar Triangle

Chapter 6

In Fort Lauderdale, Doctor Kevin Clayton, a handsome man wearing casual greys with a dapper splash of color, stood at the airline counter waiting for a computer to trace out a VIP reservation, routing him from Ft. Lauderdale to London/Gatwick and on to Glasgow, Scotland. Clayton, a faint smile edging his bright, intelligent face, nodded in thanks to the ticketing clerk.

"Have a good flight, Dr. Clayton," she offered with a flirty glance.

Clayton flashed back a warm smile and turned from the counter. Two powerfully built no-nonsense men in dark suits were watching him. Their very presence formed a barrier between him and the nearby departure area, but he acted as if he didn't notice them. He walked past the two men toward the ticket-taker standing at the entrance to the enclosed jetway. The men fell in behind him. Arriving at the jetway entry, he looked back once, then sauntered alone down the umbilical-cord-like walkway and onto the aircraft. As the door to the plane closed and the walkway concertinaed away, Clayton knew one of the men would be removing his cell phone, tapping a number, and saying, "He's on his way."

At the Glasgow airport, Doctor Clayton walked through the security gate from the plane and was joined by two different, large, black-suited men who escorted him through the terminal, creating stares from passing travellers. One man indicated the exit they were to take. Clayton smiled and allowed a glance at their faces, then quickly corrected his expression to match the gravity of theirs. They left the terminal by a side route marked *Authorized Personnel Only.*

Jack Tanner sat in the back seat of a car parked alongside the exit.

When Clayton and his escort appeared, they went directly to the car, the rear door opened and Clayton got in. One of the two escorts nodded to Tanner, and the car moved off along a private road beside the airport.

Clayton leaned back in his seat. "You part of this outfit?"

Tanner nodded. "I'm running it."

"Then perhaps you'll tell me where we're going."

"Private plane to the Isle of Tiree, for a hotel dinner, a good night's sleep, then to the middle of nowhere."

Chapter 7

His guest having left, Commander Harris remained alone at the bar, sipping his Scotch, constantly re-parsing the room and its inhabitants. After a few minutes, Koski and Falk walked together over to the bar, took seats beside him, and introduced themselves. Following pleasantries and assurances that no one was listening or watching, Falk revealed that he and Koski were American federal agents assigned to see that the scientific contingent arrived safely at the lighthouse.

"Yes, I was advised you were to join us. London filled me in rather well." Harris took a long look at Koski before continuing. "Where's Tanner? I thought he was to be the one to liaise everything. The meeting, accommodation, schedule, the lot."

"He is, Commander," Falk replied. "He'll be arriving with Doctor Clayton later today."

"I don't understand why it takes two security groups to see us off safely. We're not a group of school children, Mr. Falk. Everyone in London seems to think the security arrangements provided by Mr. Tanner and the U. S. State Department sufficient."

"Nonetheless, those are our orders, Commander."

Harris snorted and rudely turned away, downing the last of his drink. Koski and Falk watched him stand and cross the lounge, stopping to chat with others on his way.

"What does he do, anyway?" Koski asked.

"He's one of the coordinators. Administration and logistics. You know how it is when you get three different governments sending their top scientists to exchange ideas on how best to utilize solar power to benefit humankind."

Koski raised her eyes. "Yeah, sure. While we and everyone else wonder what they're really up to."

"Exactly. That's the reason they're holding this meeting in a remote location. It was chosen to be nigh impossible for the media, or anyone else for that matter, to interrupt them. Up to now, two of the three 'brains' have made it this far without being noticed. If they'd been movie stars, the media vans would be out there now with their dishes pointing high in the sky." Falk watched the blonde and the serious-faced man at the front desk while he talked.

Chapter 8

Courtney Spencer and Dr. Jacob Jenner sat at a table in the bay window, Courtney twirling the stem of her empty wine glass between slender fingers. "You haven't actually met this Dr. Clayton, have you?" she asked with twinkling eyes.

"Not yet. Have you?" Jenner asked as he peered around the room.

"No. But I've heard all about him and can't wait to meet him."

"Why?"

"Kevin Clayton has a reputation in both solar energy and energy research circles as one of a different kind."

"And energy interests you?"

"Reputations interest me." She lit a cigarette and blew a long, seductive stream of smoke.

Falk glanced at Koski and nodded his head toward the front desk where the Commander was rapping on the mahogany counter. "Stay here. I'm going to stretch my legs. I won't be long."

Commander Harris, red faced and angered by the lateness in the arrival of Jack Tanner and the American scientist, was demanding the desk recheck the estimated arrival time of

Doctor Clayton's plane. He was informed the aircraft had arrived in Glasgow, and that Mr. Tanner and Doctor Clayton supposedly left together on a private plane. Perhaps there had been a breakdown?

"Breakdown be damned. Get me the American Embassy in London." The desk clerk turned toward the phone as Clayton and Tanner entered the front door and walked toward the desk. Something about the two men made the clerk wait until they were at the counter.

"May I help you, gentlemen?"

Falk sauntered to a rack of brochures and pamphlets describing the beauty spots around the area, his move placing him well within earshot of the desk.

"We have reservations. My name is Tanner, Jack Tanner. And this is Doctor Kevin Clayton."

Harris glared at the two men and blurted, "We've been waiting for you. You're late!"

At the sudden outburst from an unknown, red-faced little man, Clayton and Tanner took half a step back. Then Tanner stepped forward toward the offensive man.

"And who the hell are you?" Tanner asked, thrusting out his jaw and moving in close to Harris.

Harris backed a couple of paces and bumped into a potted palm. "Why, I'm…I'm Commander Harold Harris. I…"

Clayton stuck his hand out to the flustered commander.

"Clayton. Pleased to meet you, sir. Heard a lot about you. Sorry we're late. Airports…you know how they are."

Harris nodded to Clayton, but cut his eyes to Tanner, indicating quite clearly the two had made an enemy.

Tanner ignored Harris and continued to converse with the man at the desk. "Are our rooms ready? We're very tired and would like to get cleaned up before dinner."

"Yes, sir. I'll have your luggage sent up right away." He pushed two keys across the counter and rang a bell for a porter.

Clayton glanced at Tanner, standing next to him in the elevator. "Bit hard on the old man weren't you?"

"Bombastic, pompous limey! Have to keep guys like him in their place, otherwise they take over." The elevator arrived at their floor and the door slid open. "Here's your key, Doctor."

"Room two-thirty. We're adjoining." Tanner checked his watch. "See you in the bar in twenty minutes, okay?"

Clayton took the key. "Fine with me."

The Solar Triangle

Chapter 9

Part of the hotel dining room had been closed off with a folding room divider to ensure privacy for the international contingent. A long table had been set for nine and members of the group began to straggle in. The first two to take their places were Commander Harris and Professor Teesdale. The professor, reminiscent of a small child, looked around the room, eyes bright.

"I wonder if they have any Marmite," Teesdale mused softly. "I like a Marmite sandwich and a cup of cocoa before bed."

"First, we have dinner, Professor," Harris ordered. "I'll ask later."

"Ah, yes. Very well. Thank you."

Harris had brought his drink in with him and took a long pull of the single malt.

Courtney Spencer and Dr. Jenner entered next, followed a few seconds later by Jack Tanner and Dr. Jenner. Spencer looked up as Clayton took his seat opposite her and their eyes met across the table. Although no words were exchanged, a certain chemistry crackled in the air between them.

Dr. Jenner leaned toward Spencer and whispered in her

ear. "I get the definite feeling energy is flowing," he said, a sparkle in his eye.

Courtney smiled, reached for a glass of water, and sipped slowly.

Never a shy person, Dr. Kevin Clayton gave her a dazzling smile. "Ms. Spencer. Logistics, I believe?"

Courtney Spencer nodded. "I'm impressed a busy man like you would know my name, Doctor."

"Let's say your reputation as a negotiator and logistician has come to my attention."

Jenner muffled a snort of laughter into his napkin and followed it with a sip of water as Koski, Falk, and an Israeli security agent took their places at the table.

The last of the nine now present, Commander Harris stood and tapped the side of his water glass with a spoon.

"I see we are all here." He paused to be sure he had their attention. "After dinner we will begin the preliminaries: a short meeting to discuss the next few days and break the ice, so to speak. Then tomorrow we will travel to our secure meeting place where we shall remain in total isolation and secrecy until the completion of our scientific caucus. But first, allow me to introduce everyone."

"I'll start on my right and circle the table in an anticlockwise direction." He smiled for effect. "Next to me, Professor Victor Teesdale of Imperial College and Jodel Bank

Research, United Kingdom." Teesdale nodded shyly and said nothing. While well known in his field of interest—high resolution, normal light Denisyuk holography—he seemed more the curious child than the twice Nobel laureate.

"To the right of the professor, we have Ms. Courtney Spencer, Logistics and Administration, Israeli Knesset." Spencer smoothed her tongue across her teeth and smiled icily.

Harris continued quickly, "Also from Israel, Doctor Jacob Jenner of the Weizmann Institute of Science." Jenner blinked owlishly and remained silent. No one could dispute that his research in harnessing and controlling solar energy would prove key to the meeting's success.

"On Doctor Jenner's right, Special Agent Joe Falk, and facing him across the table, his partner, Special Agent Susan Koski, both of the USA. They will be responsible for security here at the hotel. Once we arrive at our final destination, internal security will be taken care of by three elite security personnel."

"Agent Mordici Berne is here with us tonight. He's from the Mossad's Special Section. Agent Timothy Swale of MI-6 is already at the secure location, to be joined soon by Agent Jeffrey Marshall of the CIA. Doctor Kevin Clayton, sitting next to Agent Berne is, as we all know, the inventor of the High Powered Solar Pumped Laser, HPSPL, known in the world media as the 'Engine of Fire'."

After a moment, Commander Harris' eyes flicked across the table and focused on a glowering Tanner. "I have purposely left Mr. Jack Tanner until the last." Harris indicated Tanner, at the opposite end of the table with a quick jerk of his head. "Mr. Tanner, Washington D.C., is my opposite number in the care and welfare of this confidential assembly." He caught himself and turned toward Courtney. "And, with Ms. Spencer's able assistance, of course, we'll do everything possible to encourage the exchange of ideas and technology so as to expedite a satisfactory conclusion to our three governments' shared agenda. Now I turn you over to Mr. Jack Tanner, and after he's through, we'll all enjoy a grand Scottish meal."

"Thank you, Commander." Tanner stood, smoothed his tie and took up where Harris left off. "First, I would like to introduce Commander Harold Harris, O.B.E. Whitehall, London. Commander Harris has vast experience serving his government in various and important capacities around the world. I'm sure we will all work well together over the next few days. Remember, all of us support personnel are here to see everything flows smoothly for you three learned men. We are always and only here to help."

The commander listened to his introduction and then Tanner's voice faded to a drone as he thought back over the years, from a young man fresh out of Cambridge, to his first assignment at the Foreign Office, then serving in the Royal Navy during the war. A patriot, he dedicated his life in military service to his country and proved on and off the battlefield to be a man of honor, trusted by all. After the war, he returned to government service and continued the tenuous climb up the ladder of bureaucracy. When his father died, he left him the family estate, Blaydon Hall, in Sussex, a rambling pile that had been in the family for over three hundred years. Death taxes, followed by more taxes, finally took their toll, and Harris had been forced to sell the entire estate to a wealthy Asian and take a small flat in London. He never married, being too busy taking care of affairs of the Crown. He had recently been presented the Order of The British Empire, and in two years his retirement pension would be due. Harris' mind returned to the present. But not before recalling the family motto chiseled into the mantle of Blaydon Hall's great stone fireplace, "*Virtutis Fortuna.*" As Tanner's voice droned on, the commander mentally translated the Latin: "*Fortune is the companion of valour.*"

There was a spattering of applause.

"When do we get to that 'middle of nowhere'?" Courtney Spencer asked.

As Tanner was about to answer, the doors to the dining room opened and a lone piper entered. The strident skirl and whine of sounds surrounded them as he paced slowly around the long table, followed by a stream of waiters carrying trays of steaming food. Kevin looked across at Courtney, raised his eyebrows, and grinned like a schoolboy.

Chapter 10

Dinner was a unanimous success. By the time dessert was served, even the bagpipes sounded pleasant. The three scientists along with Harris, Tanner, and Spencer eventually retired into another room, leaving Falk, Koski, and Berne at the table.

"You look tired from your travels, Berne," Falk said. "Why don't you turn in and get some sleep. Koski and I will make sure they get to bed safe and sound."

Berne nodded, pushing back his chair. "Thanks. You're right. See you tomorrow."

Falk turned to Koski. "I checked with the Harbor Master. The morning tide turns at six. That'll be the best time for Harris and Tanner to arrange the trip to the lighthouse."

"And have they?"

"No idea."

"You sound concerned, Joe. What's up?"

"There's something off about this whole thing. I just don't know what it is yet."

"Off?"

"Yeah. These three scientists are super security risks, right? Each is tops in his field. Put them together and...who knows what they're capable of collectively doing."

"Go on."

"Well, think about it. It's been arranged for these three to be stuck on a remote island in an old decrepit lighthouse so they can ostensively come to a consensus on a way of beaming solar energy from space to an as yet unknown power grid on earth. They could have done that anywhere. For instance, the Weizmann Institute of Science in Rehovot, Israel. The Israelis have some of the finest security in the world around places like that. Why go to the trouble and risk of sending one of their top men out into the middle of the Atlantic off the west coast of Scotland?"

"They have security problems at home, too," Koski said. "Maybe the UK and the States didn't want their man in Israel."

Falk nodded. "You could be right. But I think meeting on an island makes very little sense."

"*Cerberus* wouldn't have sent us along if it didn't."

"Ever think that could be the exact reason they did send us? To find out what is really going on?"

Chapter 11

The following day dawned bright and clear. The only thing to mar the near perfect morning was the discovery of the body of Mordici Berne on the hotel grounds by one of the gardeners. Berne was sitting in a gazebo on a grassy knoll overlooking the harbor. His throat had been slit.

It took all the logistic and administrative expertise of Harris and Tanner, plus a direct order from London to the lone constable on the Isle of Tiree, that no word of the murder leaked out. The body, it was decided, would be kept, literally, on ice in the hotel's walk-in freezer.

Commander Harris' usually florid face was noticeably wan that morning as he addressed the scientific and security groups at breakfast. "The death of Agent Berne is a great shock to all of us. There is a possibility the meetings will be scrubbed."

Falk and Koski were seated at the back of the room as Harris went on: "I've been in touch with London and, through Mr. Tanner, Washington. As of yet, no decision has been forthcoming." Indicating Courtney, Harris continued. "Ms. Spencer has been in contact with the Knesset and was informed she will be advised on the future of the talks as soon as possible. In the meantime, we're to all remain here at the hotel. Fortunately, this time of the year, the hotel is sparsely populated. We must, at all costs, keep the matter of Agent Berne's death out of the news."

"Agent Koski and I are trained investigators. No sense letting the scene of the crime grow cold," Falk suggested.

"Orders are to wait for instructions," Tanner snapped.

Shortly before lunch, a British naval officer reported to Commander Harris in his room.

"Lieutenant Garvey, British Naval intelligence. I have a message, sir." He handed a brown envelope to Harris, who slit it open and removed a single sheet of paper. The commander unfolded the official document and scanned it quickly. After glancing up at the officer, he read it a second time:

British Naval Intelligence
Holy Loch
Dunoon, Scotland.

Due to lack of telephone security on the island of Tiree, this message is being hand-delivered by Lt. W. C. Garvey, R.N. He will show Naval Intelligence ID. You will hereby notify your party to prepare for return to the mainland and from there to disperse back to their homelands.

Further orders and support resources will be supplied by Lt. Garvey.

Signed, Admiral L. Kenilworth, DSO, MBA.

Harris sighed. "Right, Lieutenant. The rest of the story?"

"Washington, London and Tel Aviv have decided that, due to the fragile situation of the scientific exchange as it stands at the moment, the three scientists will remain under tight security. But first, the following evasive action is to take place: Your team will set sail for the mainland early this afternoon. Halfway, you will be met by a Royal Navy pinnace and transferred aboard. Others, dressed to resemble your party, will take their places in your craft and continue to the mainland where they will be met and taken to the airport. Anyone watching will observe eight people, who they will take for your group." The lieutenant paused and asked, "Any questions, sir?"

"Quite a few, actually. Although at this point I can't expect many answers, right?"

"Afraid so, Commander. You and your party will continue to the lighthouse in the pinnace. Darkness will have fallen by this time and admiralty will have cleared the waters so no one will observe the completion of the journey. A replacement for Agent Berne will be flown in from the Israel.

The Weizmann Institute insists on having one of Mossad's special security agents in constant attendance with Dr. Jenner at the meetings. Agent Koski will proceed to the lighthouse and provide personal security to Dr. Clayton. British Agent Swale is already at the lighthouse, and will provide personal security for Professor Teesdale. He was originally to serve strictly as on-site communications officer, that is until we received word that Agent Marshall fell ill early this morning and is being airlifted to a hospital on the mainland. Agent Falk will follow with the replacement Israeli Mossad agent as soon as he arrives. Falk will assume command of overall security at the lighthouse once there."

"With so many agents, that means we in the lighthouse, could, for all intents and purposes, be bait. Am I correct?" the commander asked.

The young naval officer looked embarrassed. "The navy has intensified sea patrols in the area."

After the officer had left, Harris tapped his fingers on the desktop and stared into space. The murder of a security agent put a totally different slant on the state of affairs.

Chapter 12

Falk was given his new orders and he passed the information on to Koski: "I remain here until the Israeli investigation team arrives and Berne's body is shipped out. Then I wait until Berne's replacement arrives and the preliminary investigations are completed. After that, he and I will join you at the lighthouse. Washington and London feel if suspicion falls on any of our group, they'll at least know exactly where we all are."

"That's nice of them." Koski's voice carried an edge.

"The meetings will begin as planned, and when the investigators and I have finished, and the new agent and I have joined you on the rock, we'll reassemble. 'And then there were ten'."

"Agatha Christie?"

"Right. Ten people on an island and they get bumped off one by one."

Falk fell silent, remembering a man named Eiker. A British soldier of fortune who had almost ended their lives during their investigations of Nevada and Californian lawyers being shot dead with hi-tech arrows. Eiker had been hired by the Nevada gambling underworld.

A little over a year later, when assigned to Operation Judas List in Vienna, Austria, Falk was horrified to learn that not only had Eiker escaped back to England, but he had been offered immunity in return for his services in a covert action for *Cerberus*. Falk had thought hard and long back then before deciding to continue to work for *Cerberus*, Falk's otherwise ideal agency, a group dedicated to doing whatever was necessary to rid America of the scum who were slowly from within, turning the country's collective mind into a weak third world mentality ruled by power-mad political egotists with their own private agendas, including selling the birthright of every true American to the highest corporate or billionaire bidder.

When informed that Eiker would be part of his team, backing Koski and himself on their assignment in Vienna, Falk's faith and dedication to *Cerberus* was severely shaken. Suddenly he recalled Tom Stewart, head of the agency, urging him to trust Eiker, saying, "Not everything you see or hear is the truth."

Eiker had died during the course of the assignment, but not before saving the lives of many, including Falk and Koski. Yet later, upon returning to the States, the act of *Cerberus* using the skills of such a man continued to cause him deep concern and he seriously considered whether or not to remain with the agency. Koski and Stewart had repeatedly reassured him he would be making a mistake to leave *Cerberus*. Stewart had to utilize the best people he could obtain for each particular operation in order to fulfil their mission. There was no one group or person who could carry out the actions needed to save the country and, at the same time, always operate within the rules of fair play.

Were they once again in a situation where the information he'd received from Stewart was not all it seemed?

The Solar Triangle

Chapter 13

A newly constructed pier jutted from the rocky shores of Flangenan Island, enabling the Royal Navy pinnace to tie up and unload its passengers and luggage. Everyone was ashore in a matter of minutes. Then the Navy craft slipped its moorings and, with the White Ensign flapping florescent against the still dark sky, headed away from the island.

Each of the disembarked passengers carried hand luggage. Commander Harris hefted his and pointed to the lighthouse.

"We'll soon have everyone settled. Once there, your luggage will be delivered to your rooms. Follow me."

A square of yellow light illuminated one of the small windows in the cylindrical tower serving to welcome them and guide their way. *Agent Swale of MI-6 has left light in the window for us*, Koski mused.

The interior of the lighthouse had been completely renovated. The main entrance room had been painted a soft yellow tone, adding warmth to the previously grey stone walls. The floor was covered in a thick layer of beige indoor-outdoor carpeting. A large round wooden table with chairs adequate to accommodate the entire entourage held centerstage.

Harris stood with his back to the table and called for everyone's attention. "I want to take a moment to introduce you to Agent Swale, who I mentioned at dinner last night. He's been here on the island during the preparations for our stay. We were all sorry to hear of the misfortune that befell Agent Marshall."

"Thank you, Commander." Swale indicated the table. "You'll each find a personalized envelope containing information and a floor plan of the lighthouse. The larger of the two recently added bunkers you may have noticed as you approached the lighthouse have been converted into quarters. Your assigned room location is in the information package. The smaller bunker is for supplies and doubles as the kitchen. The area we are in at the moment will act as a common room and dining room. The scientific meetings will be held on the second level. The third level has been set up as a communication center and the old lantern room at the top of the lighthouse will remain empty. A member of the security team will be on duty at all times, and in constant communication with the Royal Navy who will be patrolling the area. The patrols will continue until the meetings have been completed and everyone has safely returned to the mainland."

"Thank you, Agent Swale," Harris said. "Pick up your envelope. Familiarize yourselves with the location of your room and the general facility. We'll meet back here in one hour."

Tanner had remained silent throughout Swale's brief introduction. Now he walked to the table and collected his envelope, where he and Harris exchanged dark glances, but said nothing.

Koski and Courtney discovered they, the only two females, were roommates. The inside of the bunker had been partitioned into twenty-by-twenty-foot private areas, resembling a cross between a jail cell and a cut-price cabin. A kerosene lamp was the only means of illumination and heat. A porcelain hand basin and a jug of water substituted for running water. Two single beds, two dressers, and two chairs made up the remainder of their room. Smells of newly sawed wood and fresh paint lingered in the air.

"The construction crews have done a great job. From what I heard from Tanner, this place was little more than a concrete shell a few days ago," Susan Koski said, tossing her tote bag onto one of the beds.

"Reminds me of the first kibbutz I ever lived in," Courtney Spencer replied.

Checking further the two women located three chemical toilets, as used on construction sites, set up along the wall outside. At the far rear of the building, a "M*A*S*H" type shower had been installed. The information packet informed everyone that hot water would be available between six and eight each morning.

"This type of accommodation will ensure the meetings will move on so everyone can return to the comforts of their homes," Spencer observed dryly.

Chapter 14

Pictures of Berne's body had been taken from all angles. Falk had collected as much information on the agent's death as he was able to ascertain, which meant none at all. Medical examiners had done their work and the area in and around the gazebo had been measured and dusted for prints.

London sent an inspector from the Yard, and Scotland, a senior detective from Glasgow. Two agents from the Washington Office of the FBI worked closely with Israeli detectives, but, in the end, the only fact they all could agree on was that Berne had died by having his throat cut. The body was to eventually be returned to Israel; the Scottish police would continue working in secrecy at a local level. Everyone else would return to his or her respective criminal investigation agency. As far as the investigators were concerned, this was simply another homicide case waiting to join the myriad files of unsolved mysteries. All the questions and answers Falk had fielded reflected his and Koski's cover story: A tri-national governmental team of ornithologists were on Flangenan Island to carry out a study of endangered sea birds nesting in northern Atlantic tide pools. To Falk's surprise, the investigative team members had scribbled their notes, nodded knowingly, and thanked him for his cooperation. It was obvious the police had been briefed that this was a matter of multi-national security.

Falk also had little doubt that Berne's killer, whoever it might be, ultimately intended to obtain the results of the secret meeting. Killing everyone in the lighthouse afterwards would pose few problems.

Berne's Mossad replacement arrived at dusk. Agent Aldo Zaslavsky was a man of medium build who spoke perfect English and projected disarming charm. Falk estimated his age as early to mid-thirties. Alert and keen-eyed, he was ready and eager to get started.

"It's too late for us to head out to the lighthouse tonight, Agent Zaslavsky. We'll leave first thing in the morning," Falk told the Israeli.

"Agreed. And please, call me Zas. It's easier."

"Fine, Zas. Call me Joe. We still have time for dinner if we hurry."

They were the last to leave the dining room. Zas discussed his background with Falk and both men exchanged information on their experiences with their respective agencies. None the less, both were acutely aware that neither had disclosed everything.

"I'll make the arrangements to leave early. We'll take a Zodiac. It's not a bad trip as long as the weather holds."

Chapter 15

Koski and Swale sat facing a console of hi-tech equipment in the communications center on the third level. "One of us must be here at all times, night and day, until the meetings are over. This two-way radio is pre-locked to a Royal Navy frequency dedicated to us alone. Once every two hours we must send a coded message. I'll go over the details when Agent Falk and the new guy arrive. I'll be on duty here until they do," Swale said. He switched his attention to a computer monitor. "Immediate and direct contact to London, Washington, and Tel Aviv. And, here," Swale picked up a bright yellow cordless telephone, "Incoming and outgoing communication by satellite to any place on earth." He gave a broad grin. "And I mean anywhere on the planet. We could contact or be contacted from a Siberian salt mine if the need arose."

"That's some phone, Agent Swale. Who makes it?" Koski asked.

He shook his head. "No idea. All I know is that it works. No doubt its the brainchild of some top secret lab. James Bond stuff." Swale stood, moved away from the console, turned, and propped himself on the edge of the desk. His face became serious as he reached down, slid open a drawer, and removed a metal container the size of a cigar box, which he placed on the table next to the computer. "Inside is an envelope. See?" Swale opened the unlocked box and held a small circuit board up like a magician displaying a card for all to see. "The communications equipment here in this room is, as you would expect, state-of-the-art and top secret. The frequencies and the information that will be exchanged over the next few hours are classified. In the rare possibility that anything unforeseen should occur and we have to abort our meeting," Swale shook the circuit board, "this little fella would be inserted into here." He walked back to the large communications radio and opened a side panel exposing an empty space, explaining that the small PC board could be quickly and easily slid into position. "Once in place any signal received by or transmitted from the radio will cause the entire system in this room to self-destruct, wiping out all traces of our communications and rendering all this equipment useless. It would be impossible for anyone to reconstruct or discover any of its secrets."

"That's pretty drastic."

"Indeed, it is. Too bad there wasn't one on the U. S. military spy plane that was ditched over China in 2001."

"I've had my own computer crash and it didn't evaporate," Koski exclaimed.

"I don't suppose it did. But let me finish. In this case,

everything electronic within a thirty-mile radius of the light-house, would also crash. The last act of the transmitter would be to broadcast a signal that will melt the electronics in any circuit board within that area into a heap."

Koski grimaced. "Even my company cell phone?"

Swale nodded. "That, too, I'm afraid."

"Ye gods, Swale, who are we expecting?"

"It's all plain hardball security. Now, how about a cup of tea?"

The Solar Triangle

Chapter 16

From the window of a small commercial hotel over-looking a poorer section of Glasgow, a Middle Eastern man dressed in a conservative Savile Row suit stared at rows and rows of brick terrace houses with grey slate roofs slick with rain. A bedraggled old man and a dog were the only pedestrians. The well-dressed man turned from the window and spoke softly to his companion. "I often wonder what makes Occidentals feel superior to other races."

"There are quite a few Occidentals who do not even know what the word Occidental means."

"I suppose you are right." The Arab turned from the window. "This place depresses me," he declared, and glanced around the small room. "I'm not in the habit of having to meet in such places, and wouldn't be here if it hadn't been for that damn fool killing the Israeli security man."

"From what I've been able to piece together, there was no other way. The Israeli overheard our man making an update call on his cell phone from the hotel garden. He had to be killed."

The light-skinned Arab nodded. What he was hearing was not good. "No one was aware that we replaced Zaslavsky. Correct?"

"None whatsoever. For all intents and purposes, the replacement agent is Zaslavsky. Not even our operative in the lighthouse will know different."

"Our 'operative', as you so nicely put it, will have to be eliminated by our 'Zaslavsky' along with the rest of them at the conclusion of their operation." He pushed back his jacket sleeve and checked his gold Rolex. "Remain here until contacted. I will be at the Tarbot hotel in Loch Lomond. Do not try to contact me there. Your instructions will be hand delivered." He crossed the room and opened the door to leave. "And remember: The Chairman expects the results of the scientists' meeting to be on their way to Iran as soon as the scientists finish their work at the meeting. Be sure your team is ready when I send the word."

Ian McLean locked the door after the Arab left. He had been briefed on the importance of his mission and remembered word for word what the haughty man had told him: *Active ionospheric research facilities like HAARP—the High-frequency Active Auroral Research Program—attempt to induce small, temporary weather changes in a limited area directly over the facility which, in no way, compares to worldwide events frequently caused by the sun. The meetings at the lighthouse were expected to provide new insights into ways that solar energy can be used to create weather changes at the international level.*

McLean knew worldwide weather control could not only provide unlimited food and energy resources to the nations possessing the technology and the ability to control solar energy, but it would be weaponized by his client. The stakes were high. If successful in his mission, McLean and his team would be well off for life. If not, they'd all be dead.

The Solar Triangle

Chapter 17

At the Weizmann Institute of Science, Rehovet, Israel, the Director of the Renewable Energy Program at the institute paced anxiously. "Already we've lost one of our security men." Arms behind his back, he leaned slightly forward, creating the appearance of an agitated stork. He stopped, returned to his desk, sat down, and, elbows splayed on the desktop, slowly rubbed his temples.

A dark-haired woman lowered herself into a chair opposite. "You must try to relax," she said softly. "We both agree it would have been far wiser to hold the meetings here at the institute rather than in an old lighthouse off the coast of Scotland, but it was not our decision to make." She, like the director, believed none of their scientists should be allowed to be at large in a world where they could easily be held hostage or worse. "I've been assured that security will be the best, the tightest possible, and the lighthouse an impregnable fortress protected by British Navy patrols twenty-four-seven."

"Yes, I know, I know," the director said wearily. "We were over-ruled by no less than *three* governments. Forty years ago, similar meetings would have been held on an optimistic note because a universal solution to humanity's problems seemed close at hand. Now, with escalating weapons proliferation in many nations, we add the fact that solar energy in all its forms has now become, not only *the* major renewable energy alternative, but also a platform for a weapon of terrifying proportions.

"Our current situation is inherent in our political system with its intrinsic bias toward short planning horizons. We keep skidding from one crisis to another and never addressing the larger, underlying need."

Snapping open a silver cigarette case, a third person in the room, a thin man of indeterminate age, removed a non-filter Camel and lit up. "That's because by the time the problems and a possible underlying solution becomes apparent, it's too late to put out the next batch of wildfires, a common ailment among politicians. Today, even our institute scientists are not free from this effect, depending as we do on government funding."

"And so our government sends our own Doctor Jacob Jenner, our top solar scientist, to *exchange* information and plans with an American and an Englishman in a remote lighthouse in the North Atlantic." The director's voice grew louder, and he pounded a fist on the desktop. "The meeting has not yet begun and there is already a murder! No, I stand by my argument with the government. We should have never have let Jenner go to the meeting!"

"It's too late to do anything now," the thin man said. "At least, when Jenner returns, we will have significantly advanced our plans for solar power transference from space to earth." He blew a long stream of tobacco smoke skyward and continued. "Also, we'll have the backing of three governments for the continuation of the project."

The Solar Triangle

Chapter 18

Falk turned off the outboard motor and coasted the Zodiac to the dock. "Grab a line, Zas. I'll tie the stern." Together the men secured the water craft and within five minutes had their gear unloaded. It was shortly after dawn; the sky was streaked with a reddish tinge of winter light that allowed a view of heavy cloud cover. "Another nice day at the seaside," Falk muttered as he hefted his kit. "Let's hope they have the coffee on." Both men headed toward the lighthouse; Falk noted that the communication room near the top of the building glowed with light.

"I don't think much of the Royal Navy's patrol," Zas said. "We just sailed three miles across open water and no one bothered us. We could have been invading the place."

Falk smiled. "That's because the Navy knew exactly when we were starting out, how long it would take, and how many were on board. Now they know we're tied up and walking up the front door for a cup of coffee."

"If they're that good, why do they need us?"

"You know the way the services are, Zas: filled with inter-departmental distrust. Besides, we can't let the British Navy take all the credit."

Falk gave the lighthouse door a good pounding. "Come on. Open the door. Anyone up yet?"

"Morning, Joe, I've had a bead on both of you since you stood on the dock." Koski came around the side of the cylindrical building holding a wicked looking assault rifle across her chest. Zas stared at it, then her, eyebrows arched.

"Zas, meet my partner, Agent Susan Koski." Koski slung her weapon onto her shoulder and shook his hand.

"I see she didn't leave everything to the Navy. And that weapon? I don't think I've ever seen one quite like it."

"Good morning," Koski said, hefting the weapon and continuing, "It's a repurposed advance prototype of the U. S. Army's future M4 Carbine. Special. Just for this mission."

Turning to Falk, she approached and offered another good morning, this time with an embrace and a lingering kiss.

Breaking away, Koski returned to Zas, a flush in her cheeks from more than just the cold morning weather. "It's not against the rules. We plan to be married one day."

While Zas, smiling, laughed at her explanation, the lighthouse door creaked open and Agent Timothy Swale peered around the edge. "We don't want any, go away." He grinned and opened the door wide. "Come in and don't let all the cold air in. This is a damn hard place to keep warm."

Swale led the way up through the first and second floors to the communications room and, after being introduced to Zas by Koski, explained the radio computer drill to Falk and Zas. Afterwards, Koski advised Falk that the first meeting of the three scientists was scheduled to begin that morning at nine and that Tanner and Harris were already at each other's throats.

"What's the problem?" Falk asked.

"Tanner thinks Harris is a pompous ass and insists on trying the old man's patience."

Great. Just what we need, Falk thought. "Zas and I need to take a look around. We'll meet you for breakfast and can discuss this more."

"I have some good news," Swale interrupted. "Courtney Spencer volunteered to be the breakfast cook. Wait 'til you taste her blintzes."

"What about the other meals?" Falk asked.

"Ah, well, I do lunch if I'm not assigned to other duties. And dinner…well, no one's volunteered for tonight yet."

Falk grunted and pointed up the spiral staircase. "Come on, Zas. Let's finish the communications briefing so we can continue the fifty cent tour." Swale was explaining the working of the communication center when three abrupt beeps emitted from the speaker array caused Zas to jump.

Swale sat in front of the transceiver, and flicked on a microphone switch. "Hello, Sea Shell. This Beachcomber. Code Blue."

A voice from the speaker answered. "Respond after blue."

Swale ran his finger down a list of words on a card secured to the desk by a long, thin chain. "Response Code Green."

"Roger that. Sea Shell out," the speaker issued.

"Beachcomber out." Swale leaned back in his chair. "It's a straight forward question and answer code exchange." He pushed the card across the table. "It's all here. I give blue and next to it is green, see?" Falk and Zas leaned in to look. "Koski and I went over it yesterday," Swale said. "Nothing to it as long as we give the right color answer." He stretched and yawned. "We exchange codes every two hours as long as all is normal. We can, of course, transmit signals at will. The Navy is constantly monitoring our frequency, day and night."

Koski eased the weapon off her shoulder and returned it to a wall lock box. "Okay, Swale, I'll grab some breakfast, then come back and relieve you so you can get some sleep." She turned to Falk. "He's been up all night."

Falk tapped Swale's shoulder. "I appreciate that. As the new head of security, I'll make up a schedule and we'll share the load."

Chapter 19

The American and the Israeli scientists sat at the conference table with Tanner as Commander Harris. As soon as Professor Teesdale entered and sat, Tanner began. "As you know, we are back to full strength with our security personnel, and I want to take a moment to introduce them to you. Agent Aldo Zaslavsky." Tanner pointed toward a man, standing inside the entrance with his back to the wall. "He's informed me to have everyone call him Zas. It's easier to pronounce and remember."

Zas nodded.

"Okay, ground rules." Tanner continued. "In thirty minutes, a meeting between Ms. Spencer, Commander Harris, and myself will begin, dealing with organization and the strategic ramifications of this project. If we can agree in principle, then the first scientific exchanges can immediately begin taking place." Tanner checked his papers. "I have no doubt that you, the principles of this scientific exchange, may be wondering why all details were not ironed out prior to your arrival. I'm sure you understand the need for secrecy and the extensive logistics needed to get us all here and support us without reinforcement during the meetings. All possible actions have been taken to keep our meetings from the media. Not even the Royal Navy knows who we are or why we're here. Our governments have fabricated two concurrent cover stories: The hotel staff and local population were advised that we were an international scientific team studying threatened shore birds of the North Atlantic. The Royal Navy have been informed that we are part of an Anglo-American-Israeli unit, testing radio, computer, and laser communications in timed responses for possible wartime or international emergencies."

Harris put in his two cents worth. "Yes, quite correct. As far as my own office is concerned, I'm on holiday in the Highlands, studying edged weaponry of the ancient clans." He glanced across at Tanner. "Tanner here is bird watching. But between you and me, he doesn't know the difference between a blue tit and a red breast, right, old chap?"

The two women ignored Harris' sexist remark.

Tanner didn't actually grind his teeth, but he came close, instead adding, "After the details of our organizational meeting are worked out, the scientific caucus will begin." He checked his notes. "Professor Teesdale will open with a presenation on the design and function of optical transmitters, emphasizing the temporal shaping and directing of solar energy beams." Teesdale, relaxed and serene, was gazing off into space. "Doctor Jenner will be second. He will share with us his development of a fifty giga-watt solar concentrator and an attending master oscillator power amplifier (MOPA). Doctor Clayton will then present his latest advancements in the development of his High Powered Solar Pumped Laser, or HPSPL, the 'Engine of Fire' about which we have all have all heard so much and yet lack all technical details. When these subjects have been discussed, Doctor Clayton will outline a plan to combine the three subjects into one discipline, making our shared dream of controlled solar energy, beamed to earth-located bases, to be used to benefit humanity worldwide."

Courtney Spencer's voice, low but heard clearly when she breathed, "Or to any target on the face of the earth, and any satellites or missiles in space we deem necessary to annihilate."

The Solar Triangle

Chapter 20

The lone constable on Tiree had been ordered not to mention anything about the hotel murder. A career man, he'd nodded stoically and continued about his business seeing that the island remained a law-abiding place.

Outside the locked door of the meeting room, Zas was seated on a wooden chair, a mini Uzi resting on his knees. A bare fourteen inches overall, it maintained the larger version's firepower of 950 rounds per minute. Zas tipped his chair back against the wall. Except for the soft murmur of voices inside the room, the interior of the lighthouse was silent.

Swale was back in the communications room. Falk had arranged for there to always be two security agents, one outside the meeting door, the other in the communications room always within sight of each other. Satisfied, Koski and Falk began their outside patrol.

A cold salt-laden wind cut across the island as the two trudged over the rocky ground toward where the land jutted out to sea. Koski blinked in discomfort as an extra strong gust of wind threw grit and sand toward them. She would be glad when they circled away from the wind toward the leeward side of a rocky outcropping that Falk had pointed out as their turning point. Falk signalled for her to wait and, walking closer to the edge of the bluff, peered down at the breakers crashing over the rocks twenty feet below. He was about to turn away when a sea bird flew up in front of him, banked to the left, caught an upward draft, and soared high overhead, all in a matter of seconds. Curious as to why a bird should suddenly appear out of nowhere, he moved closer to the edge and leaned farther over, thinking perhaps he would spot a nest in the cliff face. Koski, noticing his curiosity, began to approach, but Falk waved her back. After a couple of minutes he backed away from the edge and re-joined her.

"Did you see that bird just then? It came up from below us, yet I can't see a nest. I don't know of any sea birds that nest on the beach."

"Let me take a look." Koski started for the edge.

"Wait," Falk warned. "I don't need to lose another agent. Let's both go, but as we near the brink, we'll crawl to the edge, then lay flat. That way we can take our time and not not have to worry about being blown off the bluff."

As they lay side-by-side, craning their necks in all directions, when Falk spotted it: the tip of what seemed to be a metal pipe jutting from the cliff face. The pipe was almost at water level amid a pile of large rocks at the base of the cliff. "Over there to the right," Falk said, jabbing his gloved forefinger toward his find.

"What are we looking for? I can't see anything except rocks and sea."

"Three feet to my right and straight down; it looks like the tip of a drainage pipe. It's the same color as the rocks. See it?"

After a few more minutes of scrutinizing the rocks below her, she noticed it. "I see it now. What is it for?"

"I don't know for sure, but I'll soon find out. You wait here. Once I'm down you can join me, but be careful."

"It might be safer if we both went the long way around. The land dips toward the beach about a quarter mile back and it won't be so far to climb," Koski offered.

She was right, of course. One slip and they'd be short another member of the security force. Falk got to his feet, looked around, found a stout stick, then with a rock, pounded it into the ground at the edge of the cliff. "That'll make it easier for us to locate the pipe. Okay, let's go."

Twenty minutes later they were lined up with the marker, moving among the rocks, and had located the pipe. It was larger than it appeared from above. Falk estimated it was six feet in diameter. Inside the pipe he noted a bird's nest. "That answers the question about the bird," Koski said. "Wonder where the pipe goes."

Falk approached and leaned into the gaping pipe but could only see darkness. "I don't know. Must have been part of the lighthouse sewer system, but it's dry now. No sign of water flow."

Koski moved up beside him. "It's big enough for us to walk in there upright and find out where it goes." She thought back to past assignments when she and Falk had squirmed and crawled on their bellies, deep beneath the streets of Vienna, through the old brickwork tunnels of the city sewer system in Operation The Judas List, and later, through the belly of the Queen Mary in Operation The Chemical Factor. The memories triggered a shudder as, once again, she relived the moments. The ceiling back then had been at times mere inches above them, almost touching their heads. Her lifelong fear of close quarters had in both instances almost driven her to panic, but she'd persevered and they'd made it. With any luck, this pipe would pose no such problem.

Falk paused, glanced at his watch, then told Koski about his conversation with Stewart about the importance of his reporting in shortly. "There's not time enough to check out this pipe further right now. We're on too tight a schedule. I'll return later while everyone's preparing for dinner. Let's go back."

Chapter 21

As the meeting wound down, the scientists pushed aside the remains of what was meant to have been a working lunch. They'd been meeting for over six hours without a break. Doctor Kevin Clayton was still speaking. "If they would just allow us, the public would be able to run a car indefinitely on solar power, cleaning the air as they drive."

"It will never happen, Kevin," Doctor Jacob Jenner said. "We both know that. Not until the last drop of fossil fuel has been pumped from the earth and sold by the oil companies would they permit wide application of what we're planning here. No, whatever we develop together will be used by the militaries of our respective countries." Jenner stretched his arms above his head before continuing. "Oh, sure, there'll be solar-electric cars, but they'll remain high in cost and low in performance until the oil companies are ready to make the switch; then it will tout what a wonderful discovery solar power is and, even though their products will cost the consumer substantially more, it will be worth the price because of the environmental advantage." His face darkened. "No matter what we do, solar power for the masses—be it heating homes and business, or powering vehicles—is a long way away."

Doctor Victor Teesdale, gazing dreamily off into space, drummed his fingers on the table top. "Perhaps there is a way to stop the oil cartels from taking out a franchise on the sun."

Commander Harris and Jack Tanner exchanged glances as Courtney Spencer inserted, "I'm sure what you gentlemen are doing here, exchanging years of research and talking openly with each other, will result in a solution to our current problems far sooner than we might think."

Despite Spencer's pep talk, an air of thoughtful depression settled in.

Tanner quickly took over. "I think we're all tired. You three have covered a large number of interest areas and technical details. I think a break is in order." He checked his watch. "It's now just past five. Let's rest, get ready for dinner, and then spend a couple of hours after dinner in further discussion. We've three days of meetings here on the island, and we're making good progress. Questions?"

Jenner raised his arm. Tanner nodded. "Yes, Doctor?"

"Has there been any radio communications in reference to the murder of Agent Berne?"

Tanner shook his head in the negative. "Afraid not. The investigation is ongoing and, due to the secrecy of our mission, I doubt if we'll learn much while we're here."

Jenner gave a terse nod in return, while Tanner scooped

up his notes, indicating the meeting was over.

Swale was guarding outside the door when it opened and the six occupants filed out. He kept silence as they filed through the lighthouse and headed for their quarters. They looked as if they'd been playing a serious game of poker for six hours.

Falk entered the room as the group was leaving. "Not a fruitful meeting by the looks of them."

"I was thinking the same thing," Swale replied, looking beyond the open door into the rapidly darkening sky. "Heavy weather coming." While he was talking, the sky turned pitch black and melded with the ground. In the distance a loud rumble of thunder could be heard.

"It's getting really nasty out there fast. If your partner, Koski, would like to stay indoors tonight, I'll be happy to swap duties and go with you on the next outside patrol."

"I'm sure she'd appreciate it, Tim, but I know she'd turn it down."

"One of the boys, eh?" Swale half-asked, half-stated.

"No. Koski has no need to prove she can do the job. We've been a team for some time and I've never seen her take the easy way out."

Swale nodded.

"We should stick with the schedule," Falk said, pointing to a notice attached to the wall outside the meeting room indicating that Falk and Koski had outside patrol again starting at eight tonight; Swale would be on radio duty and Zas would take his turn in the chair. "Is Zas in his room?" Falk asked.

"If he's not, he'll be walking round the island. He's an exercise freak."

Falk frowned. What a man did on his time off between shifts was, of course, his own business, but he'd better get back soon or he'd miss dinner. No one had volunteered to be tonight's dinner cook, and last night's meal had been a make-do affair of canned soup, slices of bread, and what Swale called Bubble and Squeak, an English concoction of leftover potatoes and vegetables fried in a pan.

Koski was sitting on her bed cleaning her 9 mm. Beretta when Courtney Spencer returned from the meeting. Koski looked up. "How'd it go?"

Courtney sighed, threw her notes onto the shared table, pulled out a chair, and, on second thought stood. "I've just spent six hours sitting on my ass, listening to three solar scientist rattle on, using technical terms that mean almost nothing to me." She rubbed her temples. "I should be outside taking a walk, taking in some fresh air."

"Better take a jacket. It's cold and there's a storm moving in." Koski squinted down the barrel of her weapon, then continued. "I put a roast in the kitchen oven, with baked potatoes and carrots, and made an apple pie for dessert."

"Koski, you're an angel. Another one of Swale's English dinners and I think I'd swim back to the hotel."

"Swale must have felt the same. He relieved me in the communications room early." Koski wiped the automatic with a lightly oiled rag and slipped it into her shoulder holster.

"Do you clean that thing every day?"

Koski nodded affirmatively. "Did you make any progress?"

"Oh, yes, I suppose there was progress. How much, it's hard to say. We only have so little time to get everything together. One thing for sure: All three of the scientists have no respect for the oil cartels."

Not wanting the dinner to burn at the last minute, Koski stood. "Duty calls. Dinner in half an hour."

"Need any help?" Spencer asked as Koski threw a sweater across her shoulders.

"Thanks. I can manage. Take a little time for yourself. I suppose there'll be a continuation of the meeting later?"

Courtney scowled. "Yes, nine tonight, sorry to say."

The Solar Triangle

Chapter 22

Falk walked out from the lighthouse for about half a mile after finding Zas' room empty. Why would Zas be out walking alone at night in the wake of an impending storm? Then Falk recalled his and Stewart's conversation at the hotel while waiting for Zas' arrival. "He's back on duty after losing a couple toes on his right foot in action in the Golan Heights three months ago." Maybe Zas walked to exercise his damaged foot. Falk had known guys like Zas. They had to prove they were still complete and in charge of their actions.

With darkness swallowing the island, Falk abruptly detoured toward the pipe, using the powerful flashlight he'd brought along to illuminate his way. Halfway there, he glanced back toward the glow shining from the windows of the lighthouse, then carefully continued moving in the direction of the beach.

The Solar Triangle

Chapter 23

Less than a quarter mile to Falk's right, Zas was attentively picking his way over the rocks, quietly satisfied with his reconnaissance to the northern end of the island. No one had seen or followed him. The north end of the island had a cove that sloped down to a beach with few jagged rocks. A Zodiac, skilfully piloted, would be able to get in and out without too much trouble. Under cover of the darkness, he'd attempted to make contact with the mainland, but the reception had been poor. He hoped his message had been received. He'd try again tomorrow.

The Solar Triangle

Chapter 24

If the pipe had been a few feet lower, it would have been deluged during high tide. In fact, when installed, the builders had allowed for the tide's rise and fall. At this moment, it was a few feet above the sea. Even so, spumes from the waves crashed and poured in a torrent over the iron structure supporting the jutting pipe. Falk's flashlight beam wove back and forth as he struggled the last few feet to the entrance and eased his way into the gaping maw.

After pausing a moment to check his equipment, he prepared to move slowly into the darkness. The bird's nest that had been there earlier was now gone and wondered if just before, the occupants had flown to a safer haven. With his flashlight beam illuminating the interior of the salty smelling tube, Falk walked cautiously into the unknown. Perhaps fifteen feet in, a sudden draft of air swept around him, and with it, a faint odor of whisky. Falk turned off the flashlight and leaned forward, ears alert. Hearing nothing other than the sound and echos of the sea, he took a long breath, and continued further into the darkness, using his free hand to guide him deeper into the iron tube.

The Solar Triangle

Chapter 25

It was nearing dinnertime. Zas was almost back at the lighthouse when he saw a vague form flit across his vision and vanish into the shadows at the base of the tower. Remaining still, he watched as a human silhouette move to the exterior staircase and began ascending. Was it Falk? Moving from shadow to shadow, Zas eased forward, eyes locked on the person ahead climbing silently up the outside stairway of the lighthouse. Sliding off the safety of his Uzi, he proceeded to the base of the lighthouse.

The Solar Triangle

Chapter 26

Professor Teesdale and Doctor Clayton were already in the dining area, sipping coffee at the table. Except for them, Koski had the place to herself. She had checked the food; it would be ready to serve when everyone was present. Koski poured herself a cup of coffee and, intentionally staying clear of the two at the table, found a place to sit alone near a window. It had become too dark to see anything outside, and the wind was beginning to rise and moan around the edges of the concrete bunker.

Even with the warmth from the stove and Teesdale and Clayton's presence, she felt cold and alone. There was something about this assignment that didn't feel right. It felt more like a stage play with a cast of actors playing their assigned roles, none of them sure of their lines.

Koski watched the two men over the rim of her cup. Teesdale, distracted, seeming almost senile with the gentle smile on his lips, folded his thin, delicate hands on the table. Yet she knew his mind and those hands had designed unique scientific devices for which governments were willing to pay millions. Or, without a qualm, kill for.

Falk's orders to collect intelligence to be sent back to

Stewart seemed off to Koski. Her previous assignments with Falk had been more action oriented and clear cut. This one was the opposite: *Cerberus* was seeking information rather than supplying it.

Chapter 27

It started to rain and Zas' anorak was soaked in a matter of minutes as he silently climbed the outside steps of the lighthouse. The person he'd seen was somewhere ahead of him, and he stopped, flattening himself against the side of the tower, squinting into the slanting rain, trying to see upward. It was no use. His only choice option to keep climbing. At the top of the stairs, there would be a door leading into the lantern room and, having checked it earlier, he knew it opened inward. It had been locked. Did the person ahead of him know that and have a key? Why would anyone climb the outside ladder in the dark and rain when it would be so much easier and dryer to use the inside stairs? He knew the answer: Whoever it was had to have a key, and wanted no one inside to see him or her.

Zas' head was now level with the catwalk that surrounded the lantern room. Slowly, an inch at a time, he raised his head. He could see nothing but the outside, rain-smeared windows and the green iron door leading into the lantern room. The door was closed; the interior of the glass-enclosed room was as dark as outside. There was no one in sight. Wise in various means of ambush, Zas crept up to the catwalk and slithered on his belly across to the door. Whoever had been ahead of him could have entered the lantern room. Or, knowing someone was following, moved around the other side of the catwalk, and even now slowly creeping up behind him. Zas rose into a sitting position outside of the iron door and waited silently.

Five uneventful minutes passed, and he decided to make a move. Walking the entire circular catwalk, he found nothing. Cursing at the waste of time, he returned to the iron door and found it unlocked.

He now had a choice: He could go back down the outer stairway and up the inside stairs to the lantern room. If there was someone in the room, it would allow whoever it was an opportunity to get away. Instead, he turned the knob and slowly pushed the door open, regretting that he hadn't carried a flashlight, having fully intended being back at dinner well before now.

Chapter 28

"Hey! Zas is supposed to be on radio duty. Have you seen him?" Swale asked as he walked into the dining area. Before Koski could answer, Swale sniffed the air. "Mmm... something smells good and it's not Bubble and Squeak."

Koski turned to face him. "You can't find Zas?"

"Falk was asking for him before he went out. I checked Zas' room. He's not there. "

Koski frowned. "Falk left? When was that?"

"About a half an hour ago. I suggested Zas might be out walking around the island."

"Maybe he and Falk are together?" There was clear doubt in her voice. "Cover the radio room while I check the lighthouse. We'll be receiving the call-in codes soon."

Swale turned and left.

Koski was worried. It wasn't like Falk to go off without at least telling her. Quickly, she removed the meat from the oven, checked the pans, and called over to Clayton, "Everything's ready. Tell everyone to help themselves. I'll be back soon."

Clayton turned from his conversation with the professor. "Right, I'll tell..." then noticed he was talking to air.

"Come on, professor, let's serve ourselves while everything's hot. Smells too good to let get cold."

Chapter 29

Falk checked his watch; it was nearly time for the change of shifts. He had to get back to the lighthouse. He could return in the morning to continue his exploration of the pipe.

As he walked back, the faint aroma of whisky caused him to wonder if, at some time in the past, the pipe had been a hiding place for smuggled contraband. He turned and made his way carefully back to the entrance, knowing one thing for certain: Zas was not exploring the pipe.

The Solar Triangle

Chapter 30

Inside the lantern room, a dark figure slipped a knife from its sheath, the blade glinting in what little light there was from outside, as Zas slowly entered. Crouching low, he had his Uzi cocked and ready. without the slightest warning, a shadow sprang forward, knife outstretched and thrust. Zas turned to defend himself, but it too was late. The knife had plunged deep into his chest, cutting one after another vessel as it plunged it's way to his heart. Zas stared in shock as he recognized his attacker, then sank to the floor.

The killer dragged the mortally wounded man out onto the parapet and attempted to push Zas over the rail, down to the rocks and sea below, but, in a final, agonizing move, Zas pulled his handcuffs from his belt, attached one of his wrists to the railing and tossed the key over the side. The monumental effort completed, he died.

The attacker hesitated, then pulled the knife from the dead man's chest. He was about to sever the handcuffed wrist, when light shot out around the edges of the opening trapdoor in the center of the lantern room. Using the outside staircase to descend, the assassin disappeared into the swirling rain.

Swale pushed his way through the trapdoor and into the

lantern room sweeping his flashlight beam across the rain-smeared windows turning them ebon black with not a sign of light outside. Locating a light switch, Swale quickly checked the room to be sure it was empty. Then he noticed wet foot prints near the door. Moving closer, he saw drops of blood. If someone were outside and he was in a brightly lit room, it would make him a perfect target. Swale doused the lights and removed his automatic in one swift movement.

Chapter 31

Falk, half way back to the lighthouse, noticed a flicker of light in the lantern room at the top of the lighthouse, then the lights go on and seconds later go out.

What the hell? he thought. No one was supposed to be up there. Increasing his pace, keenly aware of the danger of slipping on the wet rocks, arrived at the base of the lighthouse, entered, and took the circular interior stairs two at a time. He was almost at the open trapdoor when the lantern room lights came on again. Climbing into the room he found Swale standing beside the light switch, soaking wet, his hair plastered to his head and his face the pallor of the dead.

"I found Zas," he said in a whispered monotone.

Falk glanced quickly around the room then back to Swale. "Where is he?"

"Outside. Dead. Handcuffed to the railing."

Following the beam of Swale's flashlight, Falk exited the lantern room and attempted to unlock the handcuffs from Zas' wrist. Neither Swale's key nor his would open the Israeli-made cuffs. "Damn," Falk muttered as the rain poured down. "Why the hell does everything on this mission have to be non-compatible?"

Swale answered instead, "Whoever killed him was about to cut off his hand and toss him over the side when he heard me coming." Swale was obviously right. And the killer had escaped down this outside staircase, taking the murder weapon with him.

"Well, there's nothing we can do for Zas now," Falk mumbled. "Check the communications room and see if there's anything we can use to get him free of the cuffs."

Swale re-entered the lantern room and headed for the trapdoor.

Moving quickly, Falk slipped off Zas' right boot and sock. In the beam of his flashlight he counted five toes. None were missing. This corpse was not that of the replacement security agent from Israel. Zas had been a plant. The meeting had to be scrubbed and everyone taken off the island as fast as possible.

Swale returned with a file, but their best attempt to cut off the handcuffs made little difference to the hardened steel. "Forget it," Falk grunted, and defeated, retreated into the lantern room.

"I noticed a couple of boxes of tools in the kitchen," Swale offered, shaking water off.

"Fine. See if you can find some bolt cutters among the tools, then get back up here, cut off the cuffs and drag him inside. You know that we're going to have to close this entire operation down, right? I'll inform the commander and Tanner. And lock that door to the outside. Let's go."

When informed by Falk, however, Tanner refused outright to cancel the meeting. "The scientists have begun their meeting. We must continue."

Commander Harris looked concerned, but concurred with Tanner.

"My orders," Falk said grimly, "were to abort this conclave immediately if anything detrimental to the safety of the scientists should occur. A second murder is, in my opinion, sufficient reason to do so."

Tanner's face hardened. "Then I will assume responsibility for breaking those rules. This is a three-nation summit meeting. Your job, Mr Falk, is to see that we remain secure until the meeting is concluded." Tanner turned to the commander. "I suggest we get Ms. Spencer in here and make it unanimous to assure Mr. Falk he will experience no problems from his superiors." Tanner was making it perfectly clear that Falk's control didn't extend into the rarefied atmosphere of international decision making.

Listening, the commander hesitated, considering whether he, too, should show his authority, but changed his mind and left to locate her.

The Solar Triangle

Chapter 32

Courtney Spencer knew the importance of the exchange of information between the three solar scientists. Tel-Aviv had instilled in her the need for speed in obtaining the intelligence from the other two scientists. Warned by the Mossad, the Knesset knew that if there was a threat to kidnap Jenner—and there always was—it would be at such a meeting. Not even the assurance of the British Navy patrolling the lonely island and the internal security at the lighthouse could remove the sense of apprehension felt by the leaders of Israel. So when advised of Tanner's decision, she agreed that it was important to complete the meeting, even with a murderer in their midst.

Falk was up against a stubborn, determined group of policy makers. Nonetheless, he made one more attempt. "Ms. Spencer, we've had two people killed in as many days." For a moment he toyed with the idea of revealing that Zas, a supposedly Mossad agent wasn't even Zas. Instead, he said, "Why don't we all take a few minutes time out before coming to a decision."

Courtney immediately turned on Falk. "I wonder how relaxed you'd be if your country lay downwind from a country of oil-rich, religious zealots who's sole stated purpose was to destroy yours? All that has to happen is for your sworn enemy to acquire a technological edge..."

Falk fumed internally, but said, "I'll advise the Navy of your decision and have them beef up the patrol."

"No. We'll continue as if nothing has happened," Tanner's voice rasped. "You will exchange codes as usual. If, as you say, we are in danger of being attacked, we do not wish to broadcast the fact another person has been killed. The less we say, the less there is for any real or imagined attacker to act on. No matter how cutting edge our communications are, there is always someone who can listen in." Tanner turned to the commander. "We need to finish by this time tomorrow, and be off this damn island and on our way back to our respective nations."

"What do we say when the others notice Zas' absence?" the commander asked.

"Say he contracted stomach flu. Something like that. It's only for a day. Now, let's get the three scientists in here and get them restarted."

To Falk, Commander Harris had seemed unusually subservient to Tanner throughout the discussion, and he wondered if the two men had made a pact.

Returning to the lantern room, Falk covered Zas with a blanket, wondering as he did just who the man had been.

Chapter 33

The Constable of Tiree, Alec Slat, occupied the remotest policing post in Scotland, possibly the entire British Isles. Since the murder up at the hotel, he'd had a strange feeling that all was not what he was being led to believe. It seemed the orders, given to him alongside phrases like, "Top Secret," and "Important to National Security," flowed with such false authority, he felt out of place among all the big guns from London and Glasgow. The almost theatrically shallow investigation they'd done was a joke. The tall, dark haired American was the only person who seemed genuine. He wished he could have had a few words with him off the record.

Constable Slat's beat was comprised of two small islands. Tiree, the larger of the two, was his headquarters. Coll, the smaller, was located a few miles northeast.

The resident population on Tiree was 750 islanders, most of whom relied on the traditional industries of crofting and fishing for their livelihood. Lucky for the economy, a seasonal influx of tourists travelled to the island to enjoy the many amenities, especially the idyllic beaches which created some of the best windsurfing conditions in the UK.

The isle of Coll offered a more rugged landscape. Coll,

almost identical in size to its neighbor, had a population of only 150 on the best of days.

Now a backwater of law enforcement, at one time Tiree boasted a sergeant and several constables. Constable Slat often read through a series of handwritten incident books stored away in a corner of the Tiree's Police Office. The books went back to the 1960s and painted a picture of a thriving community with all the problems entailed: assault, disorders, ships in distress, rowdiness, and even missing persons. Over the years, a decline in the islands' populations had caused the police presence to dwindle to its present complement of one officer. Deep in his heart, Slat yearned to see some action before he retired and grew roses. He knew if his wife knew of this, she would have called him a fool. Perhaps he was. However, there was something wrong with the current situation, and secret or not, he intended to discover what it was.

Slat made up his mind to chat with a mechanic who had been talking in the local pub about a helicopter he was taking care of for a couple of American ornithologists.

It was noon and the pub had only a few customers at the bar. As soon as Slat entered, he saw the mechanic from the airfield with his nose in a pint of beer. "I nay have seen much of you lately," Slat said, "Things must be busy at the airfield."

The man stopped halfway through his pint, wiped his mouth with the back of a grease-stained hand, and contemplated the liquid in his tankard before answering. "Aye, I'm in charge of tending to a helicopter for a couple of Americans. We dinna get too many of them nowadays, you know." He resumed drinking, finishing his beer in two long gulps.

Slat caught the eye of the barmaid. "Coffee, meat pie and chips, Molly," he ordered as he settled in at the bar, removing his helmet and placing it beside the beer taps. It was his sign that he was off duty for lunch. "So tell me, where do the Americans fly their helicopter? I haven't seen it much around here."

Molly slid a plate containing a hot cheese and beef sandwich in front of the mechanic who nodded at the empty tankard, indicating the need for second pint. Taking a large bite out of the sandwich, he chewed slowly, saying, "I dinna know. They have nay used the thing for a few days." He scooped up a pile of potato chips and stuffed them his mouth, signalling that was all he was going to say.

Slat didn't want to sound as if his questions were in an official capacity. "Well, I suppose Americans do things like flying out here to fish off the rocks. Seems odd they'd choose this time of the year, though."

The mechanic smiled slyly as if he knew something the constable didn't. It gave him a warm feeling to be one up on the law. "They dinna come to fish. They're studying shore birds and their mating habits. Fucking waste of time if you ask me."

Molly arrived with Slat's meat pie and chips and topped off his coffee. What the mechanic had just told him made Slat even more interested. Studying shore birds and their mating habits sounded like a damn fool story to him, too. Taking his knife and fork he sliced open his pie, and savored the aroma of its contents. He ate silently, mashing the potatoes into the rich, thick gravy, loading in a mouthful.

The mechanic said, "Stop by and you can take a look at the helicopter. It has a company logo on its side—most likely some environmental group. They have money to burn." The mechanic sounded as if he had little use for do-gooders poking around the island, as they would likely end up causing more problems than good.

Slat agreed, saying he'd like to see the copter up close; he'd stop at the strip later in the day.

"Dinna come too late. I go home at four-thirty." The mechanic finished the remainder of his second pint, pushed back from the bar, and left.

Chapter 34

Swale had successfully removed the handcuffs from Zas using of a pair of bolt cutters left in the kitchen by the construction crew. Zas body lay in the lantern room, now covered by a tarp. Falk told Swale and Koski about the orders given by Tanner. "If we act against Tanner, Harris and Spencer's orders, we're the ones who'll catch all the flack. We're here as security, nothing else. In truth, we have no authority regarding command decisions in any of this operation."

Koski, sitting next to Falk at the table in the kitchen, seethed inside and she shared her frustration, itching for action. "Okay, Joe. The scientists are back in their meeting. Tanner, Harris and Spencer are engaged elsewhere. What is *your* plan? I know you're not going to just sit here and acquiesce. And what about that pipe? When you came back, you rushed upstairs like a bat out of hell looking for Zas."

Falk, sipping on his third cup of coffee, related his trip down the inside of the pipe and how he'd run out of time and had to head back to the lighthouse. Pushing his now empty coffee mug to one side, he added in a hushed voice, "There was something odd. This place was supposedly deserted for years until the construction crew came here." Swale and Koski nodded in acknowledgement. "Well, either I was imagining it or the construction team built a still down there because I got a definite whiff of whisky."

"Scotch or Irish?" asked Swale.

Falk smiled obliquely. "I didn't have long enough to investigate further. I had to get back here for my shift," and continued. "With Zas out of the picture, we'll have to create a new schedule."

"I'll do permanent radio room duty if you like," Swale offered. "I can keep an eye on the meeting between transmissions. That'll give you and Koski more flexibility. The decision's up to you, of course."

Falk nodded his appreciation. "Thanks. Then I can head back to the pipe. I'll carry my cell phone, although I don't know if it'll work from inside an underground pipe."

"Take the yellow one from the radio room," Koski said. "Swale says it'll work from inside a Siberian salt mine." She turned to Swale. "Right?"

"Absolutely. I'll go get it and, at the same time, transmit our code exchanges." He pushed from the table and left the room.

Falk watched him leave. "While I'm investigating the pipe, Koski, I want you to keep everyone together and stay close to them. Right now, I can't trust any of these people."

With the two deaths, Koski felt the same uneasiness. On the other hand, she knew Falk's patterns, and casting suspicion on the scientists and the governmental minders was not his usual style. "What about Swale?"

"My gut reaction is that he's clean, but I'm certain of nothing at the moment. It's just a hunch; we have to have someone on our side."

"And if you're wrong?"

"We'll be in one big hell of a mess." Falk said, looking into his empty cup.

Koski scooped the cup from his hands and crossed to the stove, poured two fresh mugs of steaming coffee, and carried them back to the table. "We should abort, Joe." Falk looked as if the truth stung, leaving Koski to wonder if he was showing indecision because he felt they had no real power or control over the situation with Tanner, the commander and Spencer running the show.

"I know, but we can't, so I'm going back to finish checking the pipe. It's all I can do right now," he said, slamming his coffee cup so hard on the table its contents spilled.

The Solar Triangle

Chapter 35

By the time he returned to the pipe opening, the tide had ebbed and Falk found it easier to clamber over the rocks and up inside the pipe. Immediately the musky odor of whisky again assailed his nostrils. Was it his imagination or was the aroma even stronger this time? Creeping deeper into the pipe, he became aware of a sharp upward slant for about twenty feet. Then it levelled out again. The walls of the pipe remained wet to the touch and cold as ice. Falk touched his jacket pocket and felt the reassuring bulge of the special cell phone Swale had given him.

Stabbing his flashlight beam back and forth in darkness, he wondered how well the advance party had checked the pipe, or, if they'ed even noticed it. If it weren't for the errant bird, he'd have never known it was here. A feeling of uneasiness swept over him as he rethought the course of events so far. The assignment seemed cursed. Then his flashlight beam struck a brick wall at what appeared to be the end of the pipe. Moving closer, he ran his fingers across the old brickwork looking for a hidden entrance or a concealed lock. Side to side, top to bottom, he ran his fingertips across the rough surface. Dropping to his knees he examined the row of bricks at floor level. Yes. There was a hair-wide space between the bricks and the floor, running from the left side of the pipe to the center of the wall. Examining the floor immediately before the space, Falk noted marks as if the dust and dirt had been scraped towards him. Lying flat on his stomach, he began searching with his fingers, and in the process felt a soft draft of air on his cheek and, at the same time, smelled an even stronger odor of whisky. Definitely Scotch and not Irish.

Pushing and probing until his fingers were raw, Falk was at the point of giving up when, without warning, he heard a scraping sound and a portion of the wall moved inward a few inches. Standing, Falk could make out the outline of a two foot wide and four foot high cleft in what had appeared to be solid brick. Getting to his feet he dusted himself off, bent forward, and squeezed through the tiny entrance into a small square room with rock walls and a stone-flagged floor. The smell of whisky was overpowering. A stout wood table and two wooden chairs in the center of the room seemed the only furnishings.

Hand on the automatic in his holster, he started toward the door when, without warning, the door flew open and a scream of gibberish pierced the heavy air, exploding into a nightmare of yells and howls as a face, inhuman and rabid, looming atop a large shaggy body hurtled toward him. Falk attempted to sidestep but it crashed directly into him. As he crumpled, helpless, to the floor, mental darkness seized him. He never felt the final impact.

The Solar Triangle

Chapter 36

When at last the final meeting of the day in the light-house had ended, Koski walked the entourage to their sleeping quarters. "How's everything going?" she asked Courtney Spencer, an anxious edge to her voice.

"As expected. None of the scientists are at ease with what's happened in the last few hours. There's an air of tension among them."

"What happened in the last few hours?" Koski asked, not expecting an explanation from Courtney and not receiving one. "Have any of them suggested calling it quits and heading back home?" she finally asked.

Courtney's face hardened for a second. "It's no longer up to them to decide. This meeting has taken years to arrange and we fully intend to see it though."

"Why couldn't it have been rearranged for them to meet in London or someplace?" They were almost at the sleeping quarters. After the intensity of the day's meetings and stuffiness of the room, the cold air seemed to sweep away some of Courtney's tension.

"Koski, I've no doubt you're good at what you do. But, believe me, rearranging a meeting for those three guys anywhere other than here would have taken another couple of years. Years we don't have. If we don't complete our meeting agenda, someone somewhere else will and our nations will be in deep trouble."

They entered their room together. Koski collected a few items from a dresser drawer and turned to Courtney. "You look beat."

"Where are you going?" Courtney asked, ignoring Koski's remark.

"Radio room. Get some sleep. I'll try not to wake you when I get back."

As Koski retraced her steps back to the lighthouse, she began worrying about Falk. He'd been gone longer than expected. Entering the lighthouse, she stood silently in the round chamber listening to the wind moaning outside the iron window frames. *What must it must have been like to live here for weeks on end?* she wondered, and started up the stairs, telling herself it couldn't have been much different than some of the places she had lived as a kid. She'd made plenty of run-down houses with drafty rooms her home. She'd come from a poor family. Before her folks had died, when she was still in high school, they'd had to suffer through the long Chicago winters without heat. After her folks' death, an aunt in Los Angeles had taken her in. Los Angeles had been warm, but her aunt had proven to be a cold, unfeeling martinet, constantly on Koski's back. Nag, nag, nag, until finally, when Koski was old enough, she took the entrance examination for the Bureau of Land Management, passing with high marks. It was during her period of training she discovered she was a self-contained woman.

Thinking again of Falk and how they'd met, she reassured herself that Falk had the yellow cell phone, and would have called had he encountered any problems. Nonetheless, as she approached the radio room she felt a tug of worry—as if an omen preparing her for further calamities.

Swale swung his chair around as Koski entered. Glancing at the clock, he exclaimed, "Perfect timing, my girl. That's what I like, punctuality."

Koski smiled and sat in the chair next to him, trying to cover her worries but not doing a very good job.

He grinned and jerked his thumb in the direction of the coffee maker. "You look as though you would use a cup of Radio Room Rot Gut."

"No, thanks. I'm fine. I've just seen the scientists and administrators to their rooms. They should all be in their beds by now."

"So, what happens next?"

"Joe's out checking that damn pipe, and hasn't returned or called. We're a team. I should have never let him go alone." Koski frowned.

"I've no doubt the man can take care of himself."

She nodded, but knew her black belt and kick-boxing prowess would have added significantly to Falk's professional armamentarium should he get into a tight spot. "He's the best," she said, as much to reassure herself as Swale.

"That's more like it. I swapped codes just before you came in. Everything's on track."

"Thanks," Koski said while privately still musing about her teamwork with Falk. He had done fine before they'd met, but with their skills doubled, they had far more resources than when they operated alone.

Chapter 37

Falk's eyes flickered as he tried to focus on the shadowy hulk sitting across the room from him. A single oil lamp cast a weak light in the otherwise totally dark room. Several blinks and he was finally about to focus on what appeared to be a hunk of an old man, wild eyed, hoary faced, hideous in the pallid lantern light. When the man noticed Falk awakening, he left his chair, approached Falk and roared, "AAARRRGGGHHH!"

Falk pressed back in his seat. "God almighty…"

The man took a swipe at Falk. "Blasphemous heathen!"

Falk pushed his chair against the wall, seeking any opportunity to get out of the madman's way.

The man continued ranting, but made no further attempt to strike. "'Dweller in yon dungeon dark, hangman of creation mark. Who in mourning weeds appears, laden with unhonored years'."

"Wait a minute," Falk, now more cogent than when he first opened his eyes, decided to try reasoning with the hulk and inched forward.

"Back!" the man growled.

"Okay, okay."

"And be still or I'll blow ye heathen head off!"

Falk noted a large revolver in one of the man's huge hands. "I'm not moving. I'm not doing anything," Falk insisted.

"Aye, ye've done enough already, I'm thinking." Training the revolver on Falk, the man moved back and lit a second lantern which added enough additional light for Falk to make out a filthy unmade bunk attached to the wall. Against the other wall he saw stacks of whisky crates, cans of food, and sacks of what could be flour or sugar. Whoever this guy was, he seemed intent on staying a while.

The old man closed an eye in suspicion, leaned down, lifted an open can of beans off the table with his free hand, and began to toss its contents into his mouth.

Falk shuddered as the man continued feeding, beans attaching themselves to his large hairy beard as he did so.

Falk decided to try again. "My friends know I'm here."

"Liar!" the monstrosity shouted, beans flying in every direction from out of his mouth.

Flinching, Falk continued. "They'll come looking for me any time now."

The man flung the empty bean can across the room in rage, lumbered over to the bunk and returned with a half bottle of Scotch which he gulped directly from the bottle. "Tongue of Satan." He waved the weapon in the air as he staggered toward Falk. "And the guilty shall be punished, and their kin, and all the..." The hulk loomed over Falk, looking like he was preparing to strike Falk with the revolver.

Falk abruptly extended both his feet and toppled the old man. The gun spun across the floor. Unable to reach for the weapon, Falk repeatedly kicked it away each time the behemoth reached for it. Despite Falk's best efforts, the bear of a man scooped the revolver off the floor and pulled the trigger repeatedly. Bullets belched from the gun in stabs of orange light, ricocheting off the walls in an insane cacophony of explosions. *Five shots. That means there is one round left in the chamber*, Falk thought. The smell of freshly fired rounds mixed with the odor of the Scotch, and hung in the air like a fetid blanket of doom. The crazy man rose, towering above him, silent except for his labored breathing after the sudden exertion. Falk wondered if the decrepit man might die standing right there, then, as an afterthought, wondered if his own life might end in this hidden room beneath the old lighthouse, killed by a madman drunk out of his mind.

Swale and Koski were crossing the round chamber on their way to the kitchen when they heard the muffled sounds of gunfire. They stopped, heads twisting from side to side as they tried to locate the sounds.

"They're coming from beneath us!" Koski yelled. "What the hell's going on?"

Swale dropped to his knees and pounded on the carpeted floor. "Seems solid. I've never heard of a basement in a lighthouse, have you?"

Koski joined him, she too testing the floor. "Don't ask me. This is my first lighthouse. We need to look under this carpet. Do you have a knife?"

"No, but I watched them put the carpet down. It covers a stone flagged floor."

"Did you get a close look? I mean, did you notice anything about the floor other than it being stone?"

Swale sat back on his haunches. "Like what?"

"Was there anything that looked like a trapdoor? You know, a slab with iron rings to lift it up?"

"Nope, it looked like a flat stone floor, but I didn't take much notice at the time."

Koski stood. "Right. Well, we're going to pull back the carpet and take a closer look. Those shots definitely came from beneath the floor. I don't recall any mention of secret passages, so there's no other way I know to get down there."

Swale kicked the carpet with a heel of his boot. "This stuff is indoor-outdoor carpet; they stuck it to the floor with industrial strength adhesive. It's not going to be easy removing it."

"If we can pry one edge up, we can rip it back until we find the trapdoor. Come on. There are plenty of knives in the kitchen. Let's move."

If the gunfire could had something to do with the length of time Falk had been away, then he needed help, and fast.

Minutes later, they headed back from the kitchen armed with assorted knives and anything else they could use to pry up carpeting.

The Solar Triangle

Chapter 38

Dr. Kevin Clayton couldn't sleep. He lay for some time staring at the ceiling, then made up his mind. He slipped out of bed, dressed in warm clothes, left the room, and quietly made his way to the room shared by Koski and Courtney. He hesitated outside the door trying to decide whether or not to knock. He knew Koski was alternating shifts with Swale in the radio room. He hoped she might not be in the room. If she were, she'd be angry at being awakened. He shrugged and tapped lightly on the door.

Courtney was awake at once. Noting that Koski's bed was empty and still made up, she cautiously offered, "Who is it?" at the same time reaching for the Walther PPK .380 automatic from beneath her pillow. It was loaded with a clip of Glaser blue tip rounds. She flicked off the safety.

"It's me, Kevin."

"What's wrong?"

"Nothing. I couldn't sleep and wondered if you were still awake. Sorry, to wake you."

Courtney briefly wondered how she would look answering the door in a pair of flannel pajamas at one thirty in the morning. She padded across the cold floor and opened the door. Her feet were freezing.

"It's a beautiful night. I wondered if you'd like to take a walk."

Despite the hour and her cold feet, the lanky American with a lopsided grin looked a welcome sight after hours in a tension-filled room with three socially-stilted scientists. "Sure. Let me slip into something warmer and I'll be right with you."

Kevin smiled as she opened the door clad in winter garb, but not before noticing the automatic partially hidden behind her back. This lady was getting more interesting by the minute.

The two left the bunker to gaze up at the night sky. Kevin had been right. The storm had passed, pushing the clouds out toward the mainland, and the full moon was hanging on the horizon, about to set, leaving a sky studded with stars, seemingly low enough to touch.

Courtney stared at the sky, saying nothing. The breeze from the sea was gentle, but still icy cold. A blustery gust that only a few hours before had rattled the window frames of the lighthouse now barely moved the ends of her hair peeking beneath the woollen watch cap she was wearing.

"You're right, Kevin. Beautiful night." It was the first time she'd used his Christian name and she was surprised at the ease with which she had uttered it.

The moon on the horizon was large and bright. Kevin nodded at it. "A Bomber's moon," he said softly.

"Why a Bomber's moon?"

Kevin moved in closer. "Goes back to the wartime bombing raids. A full moon made it easy for the bombers to find their target. During the Blitz, London did everything they could to try and cover the Thames River during a full moon. The reflected moonlight made a perfect path for the Luftwaffe to follow. The city, totally blacked out, and the moon reflecting from the surface of the river, was like a beacon. The Germans knew every bend of the river and, from that, exactly where to drop their ordnance."

"Were the British ever successful in camouflaging the river?"

"No." They walked in silence, following a worn path down toward the small pier until Kevin said, "Tough sledding at the last meeting, wasn't it? If we don't get loosened up, no one is going to exchange anything. You were kind of hard on Tanner when he tried to get Jenner to be more forthright."

"Tanner's priorities are misplaced. Right now Dr. Jenner is everything Israel has to offer."

"I don't know. Israel's got you."

She gave a short laugh. "I'll take that as a compliment. However, I'm really nothing."

"Who told you that?"

They stopped at the pier. The two looked out across the water and Courtney continued. "I mean compared with Dr. Jenner."

Kevin's eyes twinkled mischievously as he slipped a arm around her waist. "I'd never compare you to Dr. Jenner. I'd compare you to Diana." He nodded to the silvery orb overhead. "The Moon Goddess."

"When are you ever serious, Kevin?" Slowly, they walked the length of the pier, Kevin indicating a crate. They sat together, huddling close in the moonlight.

"When I think of nuclear risks, pollution, and political blackmail compared to underselling the benefits of solar power to the public and its endless supply of clean energy, I get serious."

"Some of us are listening now. We're here on the island with you," Courtney said.

Kevin turned his face from the moon and looked at her. In the moonshine, with the wind ruffling her hair, she was breath-taking. "Creature of the desert. You're so beautiful…" He kissed her, warmly and slowly. "Who are you really, Courtney Spencer?"

"I'm a lot like you, Kevin Clayton. I do as I please. I get what I want. Only I have to work for it."

Kevin was taken aback at her answer. "Want to run that

past me again?"

"It has cost me one hundred percent of myself to be here on this island. I didn't get it handed to me on a silver platter."

"And you think I did?"

"You're of the Clayton family: Money, yachts, political privileges…"

"No credit for hard work?"

"Of course, you're brilliant."

"Oh, thanks."

"But from a brilliant family."

"So I had it made?"

"Right."

"And you didn't?"

"Don't get me wrong. Yours is an enviable background, but I prefer mine. As an Israeli…"

"Wait. Isn't Israel your *adopted* country? Weren't you born in America."

"What's wrong with being an adopted Israeli Jew?"

"Dunno. What was wrong with being an American Jew?"

Courtney's face hardened and she inched away from his side.

A soft smile crossed his face as he whispered, "Wasn't challenging enough for you?"

Her eyes flashed "It wasn't enough." She held her resentment in defiance of his smile until her resistance at this tall American finally melted and she moved closer. "That's always been my problem. I'm never satisfied."

"Can I help?"

Courtney searched his eyes. "I think you can."

They kissed again, this time longer and more passionately. Then she broke away.

"I have a mission to accomplish, Doctor Clayton, and you're turning my attention elsewhere." As she got to her feet, Kevin, attempting to stand, slipped on the wet planking. "Does this mean it's all over?" he asked holding out a hand to her.

She reached down and took it. "I believe it means it's just begun."

Together they walked back to the lighthouse, following the silvery path of the rapidly waning Bomber's Moon.

Chapter 39

Falk stared up at the wild man towering above him. He searched the right words. He'd be dead if the man fired the remaining round at close range. "You look like the sort of man who savors his solitude and freedom. Am I correct?"

The shaggy heap remained silent, his breathing ragged and wheezy, the old .38 Webley swaying less than a foot from Falk's head.

"You kill me and you can kiss your freedom goodbye. You'll still have your solitude, but it'll be inside a cell for the rest of your life. Without any Scotch whisky." Falk watched the revolver slowly lower to the drunken man's side. Was he getting through? Falk continued, his voice now hostage nego-tiator mode, soft and non-threatening. "I understand. Some-one intruding into my space might cause me to react the same way. I'm not here to hurt you. Believe me."

Falk was amazed at what happened next.

The man pulled himself to attention, chin up, eyes front, and in a voice that filled the room, commanded, "Guid save King George and Scotland!"

Falk took the chance and got to his feet, keeping an eye

on the revolver and the old man's finger curled around the trigger. Standing to attention, Falk saluted.

A visible change came over the Scot. His eyes brightened and a faint smile curled his lips. "Aye, that's more like it." Sticking the Webley into his belt, he went to the table, sat down, and took a swig from the bottle.

"Why are you hiding down here?" Falk asked softly.

"I was'na hiding 'til ye all came. Ye sealed me in like a wild animal in a trap." He stabbed a finger at the pipe entrance and then the ceiling. "Sealed ma way in and oot."

Following the man's finger, Falk noticed a wooden ladder attached to a wall, its top against the ceiling. "What are you doing here?" Falk asked softly.

"This be ma home. Was for a long, long time."

"You live here?"

"I did. Not in this wee room, mind you. I was born and suckled in the lighthouse. It was ma home. It was here I learned my trade as a Keeper. It was here I learned ma duty. The light must never gae oot. Most men could'na stand the loneliness, but to me and Angus…to us…the lighthouse was our home. Some of the world's finest ships depended on me and Angus ta guide them. Nothing passes anymore. Nothing comes near, nowadays. Me and Angus…sent off we were ta graze in the heather."

"Angus?" Falk asked.

"Angus, Ay. He was ma wee brother."

"But you came back?" Falk saw that the man was settling down, seemingly more calm as he continued to answer questions.

"They sealed the trapdoor closed." He pointed again to where the ladder met the ceiling.

"Who?"

"I dinna know. They came and changed everything...cleaned, painted, built things. They were here for days. I had to stay hidden down here in this place." He swept his arm around the small room. "This was a fresh water cistern when I was a boy, a storage place for our drinking water. Every year now, old Lars Vanheut brings me out in his boat for ma two weeks holiday from grazing the Highlands.

"When will Lars Vanheut come back for you?"

"Ach! I've barely arrived, laddie."

Falk expelled his breath slowly. "Well, if what you say is true, you've picked a hell of a time to take your vacation."

The old man shook his shaggy head. A bean loosened from his beard and fell noiselessly to the floor. He held his bottle to the light for a moment then returned it to his lips and drained the remains. At that moment there was a rasping sound, and a shaft of light beamed down from above where the top of the ladder met the ceiling.

Falk moved fast. He grabbed the revolver from the old

man's waistband, then turned and pointed it at the light.

Swale and Koski were already down the ladder and into the room, both holding their weapons in ready position. This time the old man simply sat at the table, unmoving.

"You okay?" Koski asked, rushing to Falk's side.

"I'm fine." He put his arm around her shoulders, then addressed Swale. "Anyone else know about this?"

"No one," answered Swale. "We were crossing the floor upstairs when we heard the gunfire. We ripped up the carpet, found a trapdoor, and here we are."

"Good. Let's keep it that way." Falk went to the table and sat opposite the man. "Look. Tell me your name; I have to call you something."

"Call me, Jock."

"Fine. Listen, Jock. I need you to stay down here a little longer. I don't have time to explain, but let me say that what you saw going on up above here is of vital importance to the country. I trust you're a God-fearing man and a patriot. Am I correct?"

Jock jumped to his feet, stood again at attention and roared, "Guid bless King George and Scotland." Swale and Koski stared at the scene in amazement.

"Just a couple of days, Jock, and then you can have the run of the lighthouse. How's that sound?" Turning to Koski and Swale, he continued. "We'll have to re-cover the trapdoor; I don't want anyone up there to know about this room or Jock."

Jock studied his work worn hands as they rested on the table. "And ye say I'd be doing a duty for ma country?"

"Yes, Jock, you will."

"And it will help keep the lighthouse from becoming a ruin?"

"I'll do all I can to see that it doesn't"

Jock thumped his fist on the table. "Then ye have ma solemn word. I'll remain quiet down here until ye give me the all clear." He held out a massive hand and Falk shook it, feeling the surprisingly strong grip of the old Scot.

Falk, Koski, and Swale sat in the radio room sipping stale coffee. It was well after two in the morning and Falk was winding down his account of how he'd entered the pipe and found his way to the hidden room. "If Jock can have his pal bring him out to the lighthouse and drop him off with no one knowing anything about it, it's definitely time to blow the whistle and abort the meeting no matter what the three government bureaucrats think."

"We could get in touch with Stewart. He should be able to pull some strings," Koski suggested.

Falk shook his head. "No, I'm thinking that our communications may be compromised. Given everything that's happened, it's the only reasonable explanation."

"By whom?" Koski asked.

"Good question. To answer that, I'll have to think of a way of getting back to the mainland without causing any suspicion from Tanner and Co."

"This mission called for four security personnel," Swale said, pulling his chair in closer to the desk in readiness for the next code exchange. "We're already down to three, and you're talking of making it two. I doubt Tanner or any of them are going to go for you buzzing off to the mainland right now."

"Then I'll have to make a quick trip without them knowing I'm gone." Falk checked his watch. "It's after two thirty. The weather's calm and the moon, though full, will set soon. If I leave in the next half hour, I could be at Tiree before five and sneak ashore to the constable's house before daylight. I only met the man once, but I had the feeling he wasn't buying what he was being given by the big brass from Glasgow. Once I get his confidence, I can contact Stewart on the constable's landline. Then, as soon as I'm confident it's secure, I'll request a Fast Deploy Team be sent to the lighthouse to close down the meeting and evacuate everyone."

Koski nodded. "You can count on me one hundred percent to handle this end and cover your absence. If while you're away, the question is asked where you are, what do you want us to say?"

"Special assignment. Say that due to the mysterious circumstances surrounding the deaths of the two security agents. Say that, as agent in charge, I've been ordered to maintain a top secret radio watch and must remain in the radio room night and day. I'll return tomorrow evening. Any questions?"

"Plenty," Koski replied, "but I doubt it'll do any good to ask." She moved close beside him. "Be careful, Joe. I wish I could be with you, but rest assured we'll have this end covered."

"Yeah, I know. Each of you take care of the other. You'll be the only two agents here for awhile." Searching her face, he could see her eagerness to take on the mission. "And remember, we have Jock down there in his cubby hole."

"As if either of us could forget him," she quipped.

The Solar Triangle

Chapter 40

It was pre-dawn by the time Falk steered the Zodiac into the still, dark harbor on the Isle of Tyree. He'd made better time than anticipated. The sea had been calm, and he'd had a stiff wind at his back the entire way. Throttling back the outboard to a low throb, he eased into a tie-down along the harbor wall, close to a built-in iron ladder set into the rough stone wall leading up onto the quayside.

Ashore, he walked through the darkness, passing a small food market, bank, post office and ambled up to the police station. He knew the constable lived with his wife in small living quarters above the police station. Falk glanced up at a lantern-style lamp over the doorway with the words POLICE stencilled on the blue-painted front door. Falk reached for the large iron door knocker and rapped three times, wondering if there were any such police stations left in the United States. Seconds later, an upstairs window opened and a flashlight beam shone down on Falk. "What's going on? What do you want?" a male voice demanded from above.

"I have to see you, Constable. It's important." Falk withheld his name in the off chance anyone else in the village might hear it.

After some muffled grumbles, the window slammed shut. When the door opened, a shaft of bright light from inside the police station illuminated Falk and the constable recognized him at once. Pulling the door open wide, he said, "Come in, come in."

Falk entered and the door closed quickly behind him. "You're the American from up at the hotel. I remember you from the murder investigation. We were never introduced formally. My name is Constable Slat, Harry Slat." The affable man offered a large hand, securing the belt of his bathrobe around his ample waist with the other. "Here, sit down." Slat indicated a chair beside a battered wooden desk. "You look frozen, man. I'll put a kettle on."

Falk didn't argue; he needed something warm in his insides after the crossing. "Thanks, that'll be great. My name is Joe Falk."

"Ah, yes, the bird man from America." Slat looked a knowing look from over his shoulder as he plugged in an electric kettle the a shelf near his desk. "I'm afraid I can't tell you anything about the murder up at the hotel. It's out of my jurisdiction. Glasgow has taken over."

"I'm not here about that murder. I need your help with a different problem, something possibly far more important than that murder."

Slat's eyes widened. In his mind, there was nothing

more urgent than a murder investigation, and he'd been robbed of his only chance to lead this one by orders from above. Now here was a Yank indicating there was something bigger to investigate. He placed two mugs on the shelf, took the top off a Brown-Betty teapot, spooned in three heaping teaspoons of loose black tea, and, just as the kettle boiled, expertly tipped the boiling water into the teapot and replaced the lid. "We'll let it steep for a bit. Sugar and milk?"

"Just as it comes from the pot, thanks."

Slat, looking more like a retired schoolteacher than a policeman, took a seat behind the desk. "Now then, tell me what could possibly be more important than a murder."

Falk informed him about the death of Zas, the discovery of Jock and the existence of the scientific meeting, leaving out all the details. They had both drunk the last of their tea by the time he'd finished.

Slat leaned forward, elbows on the desk top. "I felt certain there was more to this whole thing. The way I was pushed aside, ordered to leave everything to Glasgow. That's not the usual way we operate, Mr. Falk. I hope you realize that."

"I guessed as much. Now I'm asking you to help me get in touch with my agency by using your phone."

Slat looked at Falk for a long moment. "You could have made a call from the public phone on the dock and left me out of it. What's the real reason you came to see me?"

"I need someone I can rely on. Someone outside of the lighthouse complex who is aware of the importance of getting the scientists back to the mainland before anything else happens out there." Falk pushed his mug aside. "You didn't seem surprised when I told you about the old man, Jock, being on the island."

"Jock goes out to the lighthouse every year and stays a couple of weeks. He does no harm. It used to be his home before the light was closed down."

"He told me. But what bothers me is the fact he could get onto the island despite our best so-called security. He sails out in a friend's boat, goes ashore, and lives in the damn place while it was being made ready for the meeting."

"He went out there before the clean-up crew, Mr. Falk."

"Then you knew about the lighthouse being prepared?"

"Most everyone on the island knew. Not much goes on in a place this small that isn't noticed."

"Was it common knowledge that there was going to be a meeting out there?"

"Yes, but we thought it was a meeting of orno…"

"Ornithologists," Falk prompted.

"Right. We had no idea it was an international meeting of three eminent scientists."

"Good. Let it remain that way."

"Jock's harmless, by the way."

"He damned near shot me. He was drunk as a skunk…"

Slat's face changed. "That's not like him. He lives a quiet life in a crofter's cottage on the isle of Cobb, just north of here. He used to live with his brother after the lighthouse closed."

"Well, he wasn't living a quiet life when I came across him. Who's this friend who brought him out to the lighthouse?"

"You must mean Lars Vanheut? He's a fisherman. He lives over on Cobb, also."

"Odd name for a Scotsman," Falk commented.

"He's Norwegian. Married a local girl on Cobb, but she didn't want to live in Norway, so Lars and she stayed. That was thirty years ago."

Falk blew out his cheeks and expelled air. "For what started out as a secret meeting at a hidden location in the North Atlantic, there are far too many people in the know."

Slat asked, "The mechanic looking after the helicopter. Know much about him?" as he refilled both mugs.

"Not really, why?"

"I've been doing some sleuthing on my own despite Glasgow. I've not felt comfortable since that fellow got his throat cut, and being told in no uncertain terms to forget it raised a red flag. The mechanic has been on the island only about a month. No one knows him well. Keeps to himself. He sleeps at the airport, coming into town for lunch each day. He invited me up to check out the helicopter if I wanted." The constable glanced at an old clock on the wall. It was nearing six in the morning. "The wife will be down soon, then we'll have breakfast. I'll get dressed, but meanwhile, you can use the phone." Slat indicated a battered black rotary phone on his desk. "It's not fancy, but I'll wager it's not bugged."

Falk made contact with Stewart who immediately secured the line. Then Falk quickly updated him on the situation at the lighthouse. The instructions he received from Stewart re-enforced that he'd made the right decision in secretly traveling to the mainland before attempting to contact *Cerberus*. Stewart, too, was almost certainty that communications at the lighthouse had been compromised.

"I'll order a rapid deployment team to the island as you requested. They should be there within hours—a HAHO drop. They'll take up positions around the lighthouse and remain hidden until ordered into action."

"Fine. Advise them of a pipe jutting out over the rocks on the northeast corner of the island. It's easy to miss, but large enough to walk upright single-file and leads to a newly built brick wall that can be opened by pushing on the left lower corner. The pipe then leads into a small room under the lighthouse."

"That's affirmative," came Stewart's immediate reply.

Falk could sense the excitement in his boss' voice as the man continued. "Our contacts in Oban report that several men boarded the ferry to Tiree and should arrive there on the eight o'clock boat. They are known mercenaries. Also, an Arab businessman known to have masterminded several terrorist actions in Europe in the last two years has been seen with one of the mercenaries in Glasgow. He's staying at a hotel called The Tarbot. It's located close to Loch Lomond." Stewart's voice began echoing and the background hiss become more evident. Falk wondered if they had lost connection. "Still there, Tom?"

"Yes." Stewart's voice faded, then the hissing and echoing stopped. "I was just thinking. I know you can't be in two places at once; nonetheless, I need the men who are arriving on the morning boat watched and followed. Also, I need someone to locate the Arab businessman at the Tarbot Hotel and find out what he's up to. The latter needs to be handled with utmost delicacy. I don't want local police getting involved or for the media to get hold of the story."

"I understand, sir. Are any of our agents following the group on the ferry?" Once again the echo and hissing returned, to disappear moments later.

"No. Those bastards are too wary. They'd recognize a tail or plant the moment I assigned one . I've decided to work the problem when they arrive on Tyree." The line began fading and crackling. "And, Falk, next time use your satellite cell phone as soon as you are far enough away from the lighthouse. The phone you're using is almost as old as me." The line clicked to a dial tone. Stewart, in his usual brusque manner, had hung up, but the gesture also indicated that Falk would be receiving orders to proceed to the Tarbot Hotel and find the Arab businessman.

Falk replaced the phone in its cradle, thanked Slat and slumped exhausted into a chair. A High Altitude/High Opening jump was an extremely difficult form of insertion. A typical HAHO profile was a squad jumping from either a commercial or military aircraft with a commercial IFF signature in normal air traffic lanes so as not to raise suspicion. The jumpers would exit at high altitude—typically 30,000 feet—and deploy their airfoil parachutes within fifteen seconds at around 27,000 feet. The team would then form a stack in the air, the low jumper setting the course and acting as the pathfinder. The team could fly for roughly thirty miles in formation, using compass and points of terrain landmarks to navigate to their target. Falk had observed a U.S. Navy SEALS HAHO operation, and had been in awe of their precision and bravery ever since. Slat and his wife were standing in the doorway looking at Falk as he finished reliving the memory.

"I'd like you to meet my wife, Fiona," Slat interrupted.

Fiona was a buxom lady with red hair tied back in a ponytail. About the same age as Slat, she was solid, but not fat, and had a smile that an angel would envy.

"Good morning, Mrs. Slat. Forgive my early, unannounced intrusion." They shook hands, the woman saying coyly that Falk sounded more like a blarney Irishman than a Yank.

"I make porridge every day for breakfast. Would you care for anything different?" she asked.

"Porridge sounds great."

The Solar Triangle

Chapter 41

Tanner shook with fury, but Koski was adamant in exercising her full power now that Falk was away. "Sorry, Mr. Tanner, the radio room is off limits to anyone but those authorized to handle the codes."

"I don't want anything to do with the codes. I need to see Falk. Even if he's been given a special assignment to personally remain at the controls of the radio room, he can still surely spend a few moments with me."

"Wrong. You know the rules. The chain of command has to be followed." Koski glared at him. "Or perhaps chain of command doesn't apply to you?"

She was referring to his actions in the abortive mess he'd created earlier in his life when he broke a chain of command in the hills of Idaho that had resulted in the deaths of several innocent children.

Tanner glared back, but blustered and stood down. "Then advise him I want to see him the moment he leaves the radio room. *Is...is that clear?*"

Koski's eyes spat bullets. "Loud and clear, Mr Tanner." She turned on heel and walked away. The scientists were entering the conference room. Professor Teesdale and Commander Harris were the last to go in.

Swale closed the door behind them and seated himself outside. "Well done, Koski. Don't forget, code exchange in ten minutes."

She nodded and continued down to the kitchen to make a quick cup of tea. She needed a moment of quiet time after the aggressive verbal exchange, but felt exhilarated inside. With Falk gone, she was in command. She knew Falk had been right in making the decision to contact Stewart from well outside the lighthouse, outside the range of any electronic eavesdroppers. Her eyes brightened with excitement as she sipped her drink, not even tasting the brew.

She'd always enjoyed playing "what if" games, and she had a nagging what-iffer circling in her head at that moment. What if there was someone inside the lighthouse who could not only intercept, but also send out information? Such a call could easily have been made while on a stroll around the island. If so, it would likely have originated from one of the members of the scientific group...but who and why? The more she considered her hypothesis, the stronger the possibility grew. The two murders could well have been carried out by an insider. She ran each person through her mind. All of them would be suspect, including Swale. She had only herself to rely on. Fully energized, she recalled being in situations like this in the past and was ready to kick some ass.

Chapter 42

The wall clock in the police station showed ten minutes to eight when the old black phone on Slat's desk rang.

"Constable Slat."

Falk walked away from the desk to study a group of framed photographs on the wall, past constables and groups of uniformed men that went back over the years. He was careful to keep near enough to hear Slat's voice.

"Yes, I understand." Slat glanced out of the window and down at the harbor. "I understand. They should be arriving anytime soon." Slat returned to the desk and leaned forward, ready to hang up the phone. "I'll proceed to the dock at once, sir."

Behind him, Falk heard the phone drop back onto its cradle.

Slat indicated the phone. "That was the Chief Constable of Oban. There's a Coast Guard helicopter on the way with an armed team to detain a group of five men disembarking from the morning ferry. They'll be taken into custody as they pass through the passenger check point in the ferry terminal."

As Slat and Falk headed to the dock, a helicopter fitted with pontoons came into view, circled the ferry building, and descended to a landing pad at the side of the pier, setting down softly amid flying detritus.

"What are you going to do with five hard-nosed villains, Slat? You don't have space in the police station to hold that many." The two of them descended steep stone steps, winding past whitewashed cottages as they continued on their way to the dock.

"The Coast Guard will take care of them. There's a boat coming from Coll. The prisoners will be taken there and kept out of sight for a few days." Slat's eyes were lit with excitement and there was a spring to his step. "Whatever is going on, it's big, and I'm a part of it. I thought I was going to retire without having anything to tell my grandchildren other than writing parking tickets and keeping order among sometimes rowdy day trippers from the mainland."

Slat pointed to the three-man team climbing from the helicopter. "Our Coast Guard Service is an integral part of our coastal security as well as doing search and rescue working in concert with the Royal National Lifeboat Institution. We'll soon find out who each member of the five-villain team is."

At the same time, Tom Stewart, working behind the scenes in usual fast-efficiency mode, was busy coordinating the two missions. The American Navy Seals would supply three men. Britain's Special Air Service would prove six more. Three of the British SAS would join the SEALs on HAHO. The other three SAS would be transferred to Her Majesty's Coast Guard to detain the group of suspected terrorists upon their arrival at the Isle of Tiree. Stewart also arranged for Falk to be flown back to Oban and be briefed in flight on the latest information on the Arab man at the Hotel Tarbot. When *Cerberus* made connections with the right people, no time was wasted.

The Solar Triangle

Chapter 43

As the ferry boat, the M.V. Clansman, neared the end of its four-hour journey from Oban, Ian McLean leaned on the rail of the top deck to watch the Coast Guard helicopter settle on its landing pad. Something was wrong.

He turned to the man standing next to him. "Are the others still in the cafe?"

"Yeah, why?"

"Follow me." Quickly the two raced back to the large cafeteria-style restaurant that served light meals—typically sandwiches and drinks—during the trip. McLean headed straight to the table where three men were drinking tea and finishing a light breakfast.

"I saw a Coast Guard copter land near the dock. It might be routine, but I don't want to take any chances. We'll break up before we disembark. Once ashore, get up to the airstrip, keep out of sight until dark, then meet in the old un-used hangar at the far end of the runway. Everyone got it?" They nodded, finished their drinks, and moved from the table.

McLean had trained them well and had gone over, in detail, all possible problems that might arise on their arrival.

Each man had his own backup exit, known only to himself in case of capture and interrogation. McLean's was to locate a truck in the parking area of the ferry's hold, and, at the last minute, slip into it without being seen by the driver.

Chapter 44

Falk and Constable Slat introduced themselves to a wiry compact man, the leader of the SAS team, who informed them the team would quickly, and without any undue fuss, arrest the men, and then transfer them to Coll by a Coast Guard cutter already on its way. Falk was further informed he was to be flown immediately to the Coast Guard office in Oban where he would be given further orders.

Falk watched the ship make its final approach. People were already crowding the main deck rails, wanting to be the first off. "Looks like this is where I leave you, Constable. Thanks for the hospitality. When I return, we'll go up to the airstrip and you can meet the mechanic and look at my helicopter." While the two shook hands, the three SAS men walked into the ferry terminal and the Coast Guard helicopter restarted its rotors.

Falk walked into the Operations room of the Oban office of Her Majesty's Coast Guard at a little after ten, escorted by the helicopter pilot.

"Good morning, Mr. Falk." A pale, plump civilian, obviously out of shape seated behind a plain wooden desk offered. "Please take a seat." He indicated a chair opposite his desk with his pudgy hand. "Tea or coffee?"

Falk sat, saying, "Coffee, black." The helicopter pilot nodded to the pale man, turned and left the room.

"Jonah, when you've a moment, we'd like two coffees; one black." the obese man bent and huffed into the intercom on his desk. Satisfied, he folded his hands across his well-tailored paunch. "For your information, Mr. Falk, the five men who were to be taken from the ferry by the SAS detachment didn't show up. Or perhaps I should say, were not apprehended. We know they went on board but evidently not how they disembarked. For the time being, we'll have to leave the matter of the five terrorists wandering free on Tiree to the SAS while you proceed to the Tarbot Hotel on Loch Lomond." He unfolded his hands and leaned back to allow his assistant to place two mugs of coffee on his desk. "Thank you, Jonah." He invited Falk to take the midnight black one with a wave of his hand. "Your Mr. Stewart would appreciate a call from you. He suggested you use your cell phone."

Falk sipped his coffee. "Is there an office I can use?"

"Please, be my guest." The pale man rose with some difficulty from his desk and, puffing, waved at his empty chair. "Take your time; I'll be next door."

Falk walked around, took the fat man's seat and called Stewart on his cellular.

Stewart answered immediately. "I suppose you've heard

that the five men eluded capture at Tiree?"

"Yes."

"It'll be up to the SAS to find them," Stewart said with a sigh. "I'm sending backup. If five men can walk off that ship without being apprehended by our best...."

"Do we know who they are?" asked Falk.

"Not entirely. From the intelligence we've gathered in the last few hours, they're a newly formed, soldier-for-hire group. We believe a Syrian by the name of Abu Scha has hired them to steal the results of the meeting." Falk heard muffled voices for a few seconds on the other end of the line, then Stewart come back on. "Sorry about that. Just had another name handed to me: Ian McLean. He used to be a hard liner in the Irish Republican Army. He's believed to be heading up the group."

"At least we know the name of one man who evaded the SAS at the ferry."

"Yes. I've also just been informed that the HAHO team will be on the island after dusk."

Falk grunted. "So, Koski has no idea about the drop."

"'Fraid not, Joe. We couldn't risk sending information through a possibly compromised communication link."

Falk didn't answer. He was thinking of Koski and the danger she and the rest were in.

"I know what you are thinking, Joe. You want us to go

in and take everyone off that island now, before there is any chance of an attack. I wish we could. You do realize how long it's taken for the three countries to agree to let each one look into the others' research and see where it could lead? We break it up now and God knows how long it will be before we could do this again. Plus, there is always the chance one of the three countries might later decide to throw in with someone we don't want involved. No, it has to be now. Once we have combined the three pieces of the puzzle and see what results, we, as a nation, will be able to rest a little easier. If the three scientists walk at this point, it would be like breaking up the team at Los Alamos. Think about it, Joe. Would we have gotten the A Bomb first if we dissolved that team? Or would it have been Germany or Japan?"

Falk remained silent. Stewart, of course, was right. They had to wait. It would be up to him to see everything possible was done to stop the threatened attack from becoming a reality.

"Joe? You still there?"

"Yeah, Tom, I'm here."

"Fine, I need you right where you are. Now listen carefully."

Chapter 45

Mr. Abu Scha, the man who had given Ian McLean his orders in Glasgow, sat at a small table in the window of his hotel room overlooking Loch Lomond. He had chosen the Hotel Tarbot, not for its rustic isolation amid the beauty of the Scottish Highlands, but for the ease it would afford him in leaving the country without the constricting security of x-rays and pat downs of officialdom.

As soon as the meetings between the three scientists were concluded, McLean's men, upon receiving the signal from their "operative" in the lighthouse, would initiate their raid. Afterwards, McLean would be picked up along with the solar secrets and flown by helicopter to a pre-arranged landing strip where Abu Scha would rendezvous with him. Together, they would be flown to a private airport where Abu Scha would transfer to a waiting Learjet and fly to Denmark. Scha smiled as he mulled over the plan. He cared little that McLean's men would be left stranded to fend for themselves. McLean had readily agreed to abandon his team in return for an additional ten million dollar payment promised by the Syrian. Sipping on a Gordon & MacPhail Generations Mortlach 75 Years Old Single Malt Whisky, Scha relaxed to savour the taste. The Scots knew how to produce the best whisky in the world, and was accustomed to the best.

Chapter 46

Falk drove his rental out of Oban, heading north. He adjusted the heater in an attempt to warm the interior—everything was so damned cold in Scotland—while thinking over the instructions Stewart had given. This time, Falk didn't feel the usual exhilaration he normally experienced when starting an assignment. Jabbing the tuning buttons, he tried to find a radio station with music that would help settle his edginess. Stewart had stressed urgency in locating Abu Scha. *He must not get away.*

The Solar Triangle

Chapter 47

Constable Slat drove through the narrow country lanes toward the windswept airstrip. He had decided it was time to make his own visit to the mechanic. Slat had spent time with the SAS team after the fiasco at the ferry, before they had taken off to search the wild and rocky coast around the island, leaving the constable to his duties.

It was three-thirty in the afternoon. The mechanic had indicated that he went off duty at four. Shifting into low, Slat gunned the four wheel drive Land Rover around a sharp bend and up an alarmingly steep hill for the last quarter mile to the airport. Five minutes later, he was pushing open a five-barred gate leading to a huddle of small buildings that made up Tiree airport. It had been several years since he had last visited, and he took a moment to get the lay of the land.

The huddle of buildings had suffered disregard over the years. A wooden aircraft hangar, its doors shut but hanging on sagging hinges, the windows boarded up, reflected the overall neglect. A smaller building with a sign over the door indicated the office. Nearby, an old Quonset hut, circa World War Two, was rusting slowly away. To his far right, Slat saw a metal building huddled beneath a row of wind twisted pines. Its paint seemed fairly new, and it looked big enough to house a small plane or helicopter.

Slat climbed back into his Land Rover and headed toward the office, pulling up outside and honking the horn. It was no wonder the mechanic was glad to have the American helicopter to care for. There was little that looked as if it could possibly earn revenue. The office door creaked open and a coveralled mechanic appeared in the entrance. He didn't look pleased.

"Decided I'd come up and take a look at the helicopter we talked about." Slat slid out of the Rover, slammed the door, and sauntered toward the office.

"Just finished washing it down," the surly mechanic said. "You'll find it in there." He pointed in the direction of the metal shed beneath the pines. "The Yank said to keep it washed, clean and ready to fly, so that's what I do."

Slat stopped at the office door and looked in the direction of the shed. "You said you quit working at four-thirty. Do we have time?"

The mechanic made no move to ask the constable inside. "Suppose so," he grunted begrudgingly. "Come."

As they walked together across the grass toward the stand of trees, Slat said, "Must be a lonely existence up here."

"Don't like crowds. This job suits me fine."

A large padlock secured the door. The mechanic pulled

a bunch of keys from his oil-stained overalls, selected a key, and opened the padlock. The door swung open on well-oiled hinges and they went inside.

Slat was impressed. The interior walls were painted white; the polished concrete floor had not a spot of oil. A workbench stretched along one wall, its tools snapped into position in a well-organized array. The mechanic flicked on a couple of wall switches and a bank of overhead lights thudded on spotlighting a small helicopter in the center of the building. The mechanic nodded. "There she is, ready to go whenever needed."

Slat walked closer. He knew very little about helicopters other than they were an ideal way to get in and out of tight places. The logo on the side looked theatrical in the bright lights. He read the catch phrase beneath it aloud: "'The foxes have holes and the birds of the air have nests.' Odd saying, but nice."

"Green Peace do-gooders if you ask me. I ha' no time for 'em. Seen enough have ye?"

Slat didn't answer. He walked slowly around the inside of the building, then, stopping, turned to the mechanic who was still standing beside the helicopter. "I was wondering if you'd seen anyone around the airfield the last few hours."

"There's been neither hide nor hair around here for days. Why do ye ask?"

Slat walked back toward the mechanic, watching for any signs of nervousness. "You hear about the men who came in on the morning ferry and made a run for it? The authorities made an unsuccessful attempt to stop them for questioning."

"Heard nothing aboot it. I didna go to lunch at the pub. I was here all day."

"I see. Well, if you do see any strangers lurking around, give me a call."

They crossed the room and met at the the door. The mechanic turned off the overhead lights, signalling the end of the visit. "Aye, I will."

Slat kept up the conversation as they exited. "You said you have quarters here at the air strip?"

"Aye, I do; a wee room in the back of the office."

"And when the Americans take back their copter, what do you then?"

"Close up and return to the mainland. The owner only calls me when he needs me."

Slat indicated the old hangar. "What's that used for?"

"Nothing now. The owner was going to use it for storage, but it needed too much work to make that worthwhile."

"Mind if I take a look inside? It's possible the men I'm looking for sneaked in when you were busy."

The mechanic was about to answer when Slat's mobile beeped. Reaching into his pocket he removed the phone and snapped it open. "Slat." The wind was getting stronger, and as Slat listened, he noticed several of the wooden planks on the old hangar that had broken loose over time swinging in the wind. *The place must leak like a sieve in the rain*, he thought. It was not an ideal place to pick as a hideout. "I'll be right there," Slat said softly. He closed his phone and returned it to his jacket pocket. "Have to get back to the station. The search crew is back and they want to go over notes." Slat jerked his thumb toward the hangar. "I'll have the SAS team come up and check the hangar and the other buildings in the morning." He turned and walked back to his Rover, calling over his shoulder, "Although, if I were on the run I wouldn't pick a wreck of a place like this."

The mechanic didn't answer. He watched constable Slat drive off, but his left eye began twitching, and he quickly turned his head aside.

The Solar Triangle

Chapter 48

When Ian McLean was a young schoolboy, he'd visited an aunt, the Mother Superior of a girls' convent in Belfast. Unbeknown to him, his aunt had informed the convent priest that Ian wanted to be a priest when he grew up. Standing beside his aunt, the priest beamed, and to his aunt's delight, announced he would bestow upon him a special blessing then and there in the convent hallway. The smell of freshly polished parquet floors filled the small lad's nostrils. He was told to kneel, and the special blessing was invoked. Evidently the blessing had been a dud because twelve-year-old Ian later went joined the Irish Republican Army instead.

As he lay hidden in the tall grass at the small airstrip on Tiree, carefully focusing a pair of binoculars and scrutinizing the policeman as he walked the premises. He had seen the constable wave in the direction of the hangar, answer his phone, then return to the Land Rover. As the vehicle drove off, he gave a sigh of relief. He'd been lucky so far. Perhaps some good had come of the blessing after all.

After the ferryboat had arrived at Tiree, he and his men vanished. McLean had trained them well. Each knew where to go and what to do, and went about it with practiced ease.

It was dark when McLean had finally made his way to the side door of the hangar. He didn't have to knock. The door immediately opened a few inches, and a voice bade him enter. His men were all there. None had been challenged in any way.

"Everything arrive as promised?" McLean asked. A flickering oil lamp set on an old wooden crate dimly lit the dark expanse, creating long shadows that danced on the faces of the assembled men.

"Yes," a man named Shaun answered. "The mechanic has done a fine job." That meant the guns, ammunition, and three rocket launchers had made their journey safely via private planes. Thanks to the open borders of the European Union, flying in and out of one another's landing strips had become no problem.

"Where is he?" McLean asked.

"In his quarters," Shaun replied. "He's sticking to his regular routine as you ordered. He said the local constable had visited and said he planned to contact the SAS team to check this hangar out in the morning."

"Good. We'll be gone long before daylight. Now get the rocket launchers; I want everyone to be able to strip them down and put them back together blindfolded."

Two men went into the darkness of the hangar and returned with three long wooden boxes. McLean watched as the lids were pried from the boxes, revealing in each box a Russian-made B40 Rocket Propelled Grenade. RPGs had proven around the world in wars and skirmishes to be a reliable, highly effective and comparatively easy-to-use instrument of destruction. An RPG, portable and lightweight, was able to hurl a shaped charge with deadly accuracy up to 800+ yards. Used against the lighthouse, they could hit and destroy the lantern room while his group rushed the cylindrical tower. The plan hinged on speed of attack and the action of the informer inside the building. For a moment, McLean's mind flashed to the inside operative. It seemed ironic that, while he and the inside operative had both committed treason for money, the informer would soon forfeit his life at McLean's hand, while he, McLean, lived.

The Solar Triangle

Chapter 49

At 30,000 feet, six men dropped from an unmarked jet and plummeted to 27,000 feet through freezing cold, thin air, before deploying their parasails into a military stack formation. Turning west by northwest, they then began the thirty mile descent to Flangenan Lighthouse. Their timing was perfect. They silently descended and landed just after day turned to night.

Koski was unaware of the landings as she finished the latest code exchange. Glancing at the clock, she knew that the meeting, unless it ran overtime, would break for the evening meal. Quickly, she left the radio room, being sure to lock the door behind her. She didn't want Tanner poking around looking for Falk. She headed for the kitchen, thinking she'd check on Jock later.

The smell of potatoes and cabbage reached her before she even got to the kitchen. Swale had prepared the dinner. Bubble and Squeak again.

She sliced some bread, made herself a cheese sandwich and poured herself a cup of coffee.

Fifteen minutes later, the rest of entourage filed into the kitchen and a wail of protest arose from Tanner, Spencer, and

Jenner. Professor Teesdale and the commander had no complaints and helped themselves, heaping their plates along with Swale.

"I don't know how they can eat the stuff," Courtney Spencer exclaimed, rummaging through a cupboard and finding a box of powdered eggs. "Scrambled eggs anyone?"

"Fine," Kevin Clayton said. "I'll make some toast."

"We could take a little walk afterwards," Courtney said, pouring water into the powdered eggs in a bowl. "Good for the digestion," Kevin grunted as Dr. Jenner edged in to look through the cupboard and try to find something that would serve him for his dinner. Mr. Tanner sat at the table, nursing a mug of coffee, saying nothing.

After eating, Kevin stood in the outside doorway, staring into the darkness.

"Must have been the scrumptious meal you ate."

Kevin turned at the sound of Courtney's voice. "Oh, right."

"Perhaps I should have said you looked sexy framed in the doorway, staring off toward the sea. I have a great idea: Let's elope to the other side of the island, hmmm?"

Kevin smiled. "It would never last."

"We don't have to rush into things. Say tomorrow, after the last meeting?" She moved closer to Kevin, her eyes on his lips. As she leaned in to kiss him, and the Professor squeezed between them.

"Doctor Clayton, I must talk to you," Professor Teesdale said.

"We're busy," Courtney complained.

Kevin turned his attention from Courtney to the Professor. "What is it?"

Courtney, bridling at the Professor's timing, marched away a calculated distance and waited to get back to the business at hand.

The Professor whispered, "Mr. Swale would like to see you soon as possible, but not when Mr. Tanner is around."

"Okay. Tell him to meet me in my room in five minutes. Tanner will be in the kitchen, fixing himself a meal."

The Professor nodded and moved toward the sleeping quarters. As he did, Courtney strolled back to Kevin. "Get a better offer?"

Kevin slipped his arms around her. "Sure. A warm, peaceful deserted cove accessible only by helicopter. There, a small hut, champagne chilling in the sea, and you can suntan all over for about a month. Wanna?"

"Will you take your wife along?"

"No wife. I figure you like to sunbathe a lot."

"I like to burn."

"Then relax a while. I'll get back to you as soon as I've seen Swale, okay?" They brushed lips. She nodded and headed for the sleeping bunker.

At the far northern end of the island, six paratroopers deployed under cover of the darkness to pre-arranged positions close to the lighthouse and dug in.

Outside Kevin Cayton's room, Swale tapped gently on the door.

"It's open. Come in."

"Thanks. I need to talk to you privately."

"What's up?" asked Kevin, pulling out a chair and pushing it toward Swale. "Not another murder, I hope?"

"Oh, no. As you might already know, Joe Falk is on special radio room duty for the next twenty-four hours. Security has been heightened since the murders. Agent Koski and I are on double duty, which in itself is no problem. However, it was decided you should be advised of the possibility of an attack on this location by persons unknown. The decision was made because you are youngest and the most physically fit, making you best person to defend the others."

Kevin sighed and leaned forward. "How long has Falk been gone?"

Swale attempted to cover his surprise. "What do you mean, Doctor?"

"Give me a break, Swale. If he were here, he'd be telling me, not you. Anyone could sit up there waiting to answer the radio or whatever it is you do in there."

Swale sighed. "Okay. Falk left for the mainland before dawn. We can't trust our communications here at the lighthouse. It's possible we're being tapped. Falk's gone to contact the authorities from the police station on Tiree."

"You believe there's someone here on the island who's part of a plot to steal the results of our meetings?"

"We do, and we believe that person is right here in the lighthouse."

Kevin nodded, his face taking on a serious frown. "Do you have a suspect?"

"I can't answer that."

"Meaning you have no idea."

"Doctor, I have given you more information already than I should have, and in the process am taking quite a risk. Let it be enough to say that I would appreciate it if you keep our little talk to yourself, and be ready to act if I call on you in an emergency."

"I'll be ready." Pushing back his chair, Kevin gave a two-finger salute. "Thanks for the warning."

Courtney, sitting alone in the kitchen and nursing a cup of coffee, looked up as Kevin entered. "What was that all about?"

He sat opposite her, elbows on the table, hands together, his knuckles forming a resting place for his chin. "Swale wanted to assure me everything was under control even though Falk has to remain in the radio room and monitor all incoming and outgoing communications."

"He's supposed to be charge, I thought," Courtney said.

"He is. That's why he has to be responsible for all communications."

Courtney snorted. "Sounds fishy to me. I'll be glad when we no longer need all the secret code stuff." Pouting, she said, "We've another meeting starting in ten minutes. Let's hope further progress is made."

"I'll do my part. I definitely feel in need of some sun. Scotland in November is no place to linger."

"We both could use some sun, Kevin." She slid her hand across the table. He took it gently, raising her fingertips to his lips.

The moment was broken when Doctor Jenner and Professor Teesdale rushed in carrying heavy folders beneath their arms.

Jenner asked, "Are you ready, Doctor? I think we're going to make progress tonight."

Courtney grinned at Kevin. "Progress is our most important product."

Tanner was already in the meeting room when the others filed in. He'd been quiet since his outburst with Falk. "Has anybody seen Commander Harris?" he asked, noting the commander's absence.

Swale poked his head through the door. "He'll be right along, Mr. Tanner. He's, err…indisposed."

Tanner glared. "No doubt by that dammed Squeaky Bubble, or whatever that vile dinner concoction is called."

"That's Bubble and Squeak, Mr. Tanner. I don't think that's the problem. I've been eating B&S all my life. It's good for you." Tanner said nothing. Instead, he pushed his papers around and scowled. A minute later the commander entered, looking white around the gills.

"Are you alright, Commander?" Courtney asked.

"Yes, yes, of course, I'll be fine. Must have been something I ate."

Tanner cut a glance to Swale, still peeking in the doorway. "That will be all, Swale. Please shut the door."

Swale raised his eyebrows, pulled his head out of the room and slowly closed the door.

The Solar Triangle

Chapter 50

Falk was driving through the tiny village of Luss as darkness engulfed the Lowlands. A few more miles and he would be at the Tarbot. To his right, he could already see the waters of the Loch glinting through the trees, and wished he had the time to explore the countryside and try his luck at salmon fishing. It was not to be. His job was to hunt, not fish, and his quarry was wily, a man who carefully took every precaution to assure he was safe at all times. Men like Abu Scha didn't take chances.

His tires began crunching as Falk drove up the gravel hotel driveway toward the front entrance. Lights glowed from inside the building as he pulled to a stop at the bottom of the steps leading to the main entrance.

A doorman appeared at the driver's side. "Good evening, sir." He opened the car door for Falk.

Another uniformed employee appeared behind the boot. "Luggage, sir?"

Falk nodded in the negative, scooped his case from the passenger seat, and handed the keys to a uniformed parking attendant who seemed to appear from nowhere to take the keys and hand Falk his stub.

Falk ascended the steps and entered the hotel. On entering, he was instantly immersed in an atmosphere of comfort and ease. Rich wood panelling, thick carpets, glowing brass and the faint aroma of pipe and cigar smoke.

"Good evening, sir," a cheerful desk clerk said. "Have you a reservation, sir?"

"No. Is that a problem?"

"Not at all, sir. From this time of the year until Christmas and Hogmanay, we have plenty of room."

"Hogmanay?" Falk asked.

The clerk grinned. "New Year, sir."

"Of course." Falk signed in, took his key, and scanned the foyer for any sign of a Middle Eastern man. What he noticed instead was two beautiful Middle Eastern women sitting together at a table in the bar, their faces hidden behind sheer hajibs. They were facing out toward the main entrance. At once, an alarm rose from within. They were obviously part of Abu Scha's entourage. Falk could feel their eyes following him as he crossed the thick carpet to the wrought iron elevator. He waited as the cage slowly descended to the ground floor. Denying himself the urge to look back, he entered the antique elevator, pushed the third floor button, and stared upward through the iron latticework of the cage as the pulleys and cables hauled him upward.

Upon entering his room, Falk carried out a drill he always did when checking into a hotel. He inspected the windows. They were old-style, sash opening. Checking them more carefully, he ascertained they opened and moved with ease. There was no warping of the jamb to impair the movement. Then he moved to the bed. Off came the sheets and bedcover; everything down to the bare mattress. He had observed years ago that some cases of a person falling asleep while smoking in bed that had been written off as a death by misadventure were sometimes far from the truth, especially in the world of espionage. A transmitter or timer could easily activate an ignition device hidden under or in the bed. This sort of attack was intricate but foolproof. The victim was given an opiate, either by drink, food, or a barely discernible prick through the skin. The opiate would circulate through the body, taking delayed effect when the person was asleep in bed. The drug would settle in the brain stem and, in effect, block the breathing reflex. When the ignition device was activated, the bed would be alight in seconds. By the time the fire was discovered and put out, the occupant and device would be little more than ash mixed with ashes.

Satisfied he was not destined to die that night in bed, Falk checked the door and checked the two locks and chain. Nonetheless, he slid a chair over to the door and eased the back beneath the door knob to be sure it fit snug, assuring himself of one of the oldest and yet most perfect defenses against a silent entry. A quick check of the amenities left him confident that his Scottish hotel room had not been altered, and he decided to go down to the bar, get a sandwich and drink, and see if anything futher developed. He wanted to observe the Syrian in an atmosphere of relaxation, to better know him and his habits.

Falk ordered a ham sandwich and a Glencoe. No ice.

The wall clock behind the bar, half hidden by the head of a huge Highland Stag, chimed a fifteen minutes before seven in the evening.

Chapter 51

Abu Scha was fully aware that he was being followed since returning from his meeting with McLean in Glasgow. He also knew that no attempt to arrest him would take place. He was marked to die and his body to vanish, but only after his pursuers learned his ultimate purpose. He understood the game perfectly. He used the same defensive tactics for years, surrounding himself with the best bodyguards that Syria could supply. He had no intention of being killed by some simpleminded Westerner and having his body dumped into a bottomless Scottish loch.

Abu Scha stared at the man sitting in the easy chair facing him. The chairs were placed on either side of a blazing fire burning in the stone hearth in his suite. "Have we seen this man before?"

"No."

"Then he could be a hotel guest, and nothing more."

"That is possible, but I think not. He matches a description McLean phoned to me of one of the men waiting to arrest his team at the dock at Tiree."

Abu Scha nodded and slowly swirled his brandy, watching the reflections of the flames from the fire dance in the dark gold liquid. "Your intuition has always been right in the past. I want you to bring him here to me."

Falk finished a light meal in the hotel dining room at nine o'clock. The waiter had informed him that many of the guests had gone down to the Loch to view the full moon. The view of Loch Lomond, he boasted, was magnificent. He also assured Falk that the pathway to the Loch was well maintained and lighted, so Falk decided to check it out. There was always the possibility that Abu Scha might be among the onlookers. First, however, he'd return to his room to put on a warm jacket.

The hallway was empty when he left the elevator and started toward his room situated about half way down the long carpeted corridor. Falk was deep in thought, wondering how Koski and the others were faring at the lighthouse when around the corner came the two beautiful Middle Eastern women he'd seen in the bar when he'd first arrived. Though their faces were still hidden beneath sheer hajibs, they were clearly laughing and talking. One, Falk noticed, was wearing a knee-length rather than the usual full skirt, showing a stunning pair of legs. Before he could wonder why the shorter skirt, the woman wearing it made a kung fu move too fast to see and Falk found himself flat on the floor with Short Skirt sitting on his face. She wore no underwear. The shock was more effective than any karate blow he had been taught to fend off at Quantico. The second woman knelt, smiled at him behind her hajib and slipped a hypodermic needle into his neck vein.

Supporting Falk between them as if he'd had too much to drink, the two women half-carried, half-dragged him down the hall to the elevator.

It was an hour before Falk opened his eyes to stare at a blurry room. He had a dull hangover-like headache, and he winced when he touched a sore spot on the side of his neck. Where was he? Slowly his memory of the occurrence in the hallway came back, and he sat up stiffly, causing his head to swim. He told himself his memory of the one woman sitting naked on his face hadn't happened. It must have been a dream, a drug induced hallucination. He rubbed his aching temples and focused his eyes straight ahead. The two ladies of the East, dressed now in matching silken pajamas and head scarves, were lounging comfortably across the room on a couch in what clearly must be Abu Scha's suite.

"Good evening, Mr. Falk. I hope you are feeling better," a silky Middle Eastern woman's voice said from one side of the chair in which he was sitting.

Turning his head toward the sound of the woman's voice, he saw her framed in the doorway, her red and black pajama suit dramatic against her pale skin. *Was she the one?* he wondered.

"Mr. Scha would like to speak with you," she said, pointing a slender finger at a closed door located across the room. "There is a bathroom, there. Perhaps you would like to refresh yourself first?"

"Who are you? Where am I? How do you know my name?"

"Too many questions, Mr. Falk. Take your time, and as soon as you are ready, please join us in the sitting room." The two woman on the couch having risen and positioned themselves on either side of Falk's chair, the woman in the doorway smiled and slowly closed the door behind her, leaving Falk even more dazed.

Fumbling through his pockets, he found he had been cleaned out: His wallet and weapon were gone. He was supposed to locate and surveille Abu Scha, and here he was Scha's prisoner. He knew unless he got out of this situation fast, he would end up being killed and his body never found. Staggering to his feet, he groggily crossed to the bathroom with assistance, and, the two women leaving, turned on the cold tap and splashed the icy water on his face.

Chapter 52

Swale relinquished his chair outside the meeting to Koski saying, "After I've completed the signal, I'll return. Then you can nip off to bed and get some sleep. Falk won't be back for hours."

"I have to bring Jock some hot food. The guy's been living on whisky and baked beans."

"That's his normal diet by the looks of him," Swale replied as he headed up the stairs.

Koski sat in the chair and tilted its back against the wall, balancing her Uzi across her lap. Swale was right. It would be at least several more hours before Falk returned.

Two murders, a crazy drunken Scotsman, a group of single-minded scientists being coached by three bureaucrats in a lonely lighthouse, all together added up to the worst assignment she had ever taken on. What had Stewart been thinking to send them on this mission? Was Falk correct when he brought up the possibility they'd been sent to discover something *Cerberus* didn't know? *Cerberus* was a well-informed agency, but…

The door to the meeting room suddenly flung open, and the commander came rushing out, one hand over his mouth and the other holding his stomach. He continued his headlong dash toward living quarters without a word. Koski turned and looked into the room. Tanner waved his hand in an "It's okay" sign, so she closed the door, wondering if this was yet another incident that would slow down the increasingly laggard schedule.

Ten minutes later, Swale returned from the radio room, and Koski informed him about the sudden exit of the commander, who she'd not seen since.

"I'll go and check. Sounds like something he ate. Be right back."

Swale found the commander in his room, the bedsheet pulled up under his chin, his pale face drenched in sweat. "Don't bother me now, Swale, I feel awful. Just go away and let me try to get some sleep."

Swale backed out of the room and softly closed the door. "He's in bed," Swale relayed to Koski a minute later. "He told me to buzz off."

"It's a wonder Tanner didn't call a break." She paused. "Then again, maybe not. They seem to be lagging behind. They better reach concensus and start working together on a plan, or it'll be time to return to the mainland."

"I doubt they'll quit before they get everything sorted out. They're already past the point of no return. They'll complete everything, even if they have to go into overtime."

"Fine with me," Koski sighed, checking her watch. "But I wish they'd get a move on. I still need to check on Jock before I can get some sleep."

"Stay where you are. I'll check him out. He's most likely passed out by this time of the night anyway. Be sure to cover the trapdoor after I go down. We should have made a peep hole so whoevers using it could check to make sure the coast is clear first."

"Good point. As we don't have a peephole, it might be better," Koski suggested, "if you returned here by exiting the pipe and walking across the island. That way, you won't have to worry if anyone hears you rapping on the trapdoor to come in, and, in the meantime, if anyone asks for you, I can say you're out patrolling the perimeter."

"Sounds good. I'll do that." Swale and Koski quickly went to the trapdoor and in seconds he was gone. Pulling the thick carpeting back into position and returning to her chair, she could hear the steady murmur of voices from inside the meeting room. Things seemed to be moving along better without the commander.

The Solar Triangle

Chapter 53

As he closed the trapdoor above him, Swale knew Jock was gone. The room still smelled strongly of whisky, but only one of the oil lamps was burning, the flame barely flickering, its fuel empty. Sweeping his flashlight beam around the squalid room, he noted a splash of blood on the table. Lowering the beam, he traced a line of drops across the room and into the pipe, knowing instantly that Jock had been taken by force. Whoever had entered the room evidently had gotten the drop on the old Scot; there was nothing to indicate a fight. There was also no indication as to who had taken Jock or why. Swale decided to follow the blood trail.

Checking his weapon and easing off the safety, he turned off his flashlight, took off his shoes, tied the laces together, and hung them around his neck. Creeping through the door and into the pipe, his socks were soaked within seconds, and before he'd crept twenty feet, his legs felt numb up to his knees from the cold. Every five feet or so, he stopped, straining to hear the slightest sound, but except for the occasional splash of dripping water and the faint roar of the distant ocean, all was silent. Step by step, he moved forward, feeling his way with his fingers along the rounded wall. Some distance further, the sound of surf abruptly increased, and he knew he must be getting close to where the pipe opened. Then he remembered Falk telling him the pipe jutted out over the water, and that, depending on the tide, it would be either close to the surface, at most, fifteen feet or so above the waves.

The sharp tang of salt-laden air suddenly swirled around him. He was close to the entrance. It was still pitch black as he creeped forward, using his feet as sensors, carefully testing and retesting each inch of footing until he could hear the wind gusting around the mouth of the pipe. He wanted to snap on his flashlight but knew he had to proceed in the darkness. He had no idea what was out there. He felt the toes of one foot grasp the rim of the pipe, and he stopped still, then lowered to his knees. His eyes had accustomed themselves to the darkness during the long, slow journey to the sea and now he could see the waves foaming white as they smashed onto the rocks below. He estimated the water to be about ten feet below him. Falk had climbed up the rocks to enter; now he would have to clamber down in almost total blackness.

Swale replaced his shoes, knowing the danger of cutting his feet on the rocks. Facing backwards, face into the pipe, he slid out of the tube, his feet searching. Finding a foothold on a hard section of rock, he gingerly lowered his weight, at the same time keeping a firm grip on the lip of the duct. The ledge held. Slowly, a few inches at a time, he clambered over the slippry rocks to the beach and stopped to find his bearings. He could have saved his time and effort because a brilliant beam of light struck him full in the face.

"Stay where you are and don't move." The glare of the light removed what little night vision he'd had. The light blinding him was industrial strength; and that informed him that whoever was directing the beam was a professional who knew his business.

"Hands on the top of your head. Slowly." The voice had a definite American accent. Without warning, an arm slid around his neck and held him in a vice-like grip, while a second person scrambled across the rocks. The voice of the second man was in his ear and very English. "Make a wrong move, chum, and I'll break your bloody neck."

The Solar Triangle

Chapter 54

"Well, Mr. Falk, please sit down." Abu Scha indicated an armchair facing his and watched as Falk, hands cuffed behind his back, lowered into the wingback chair. "I'm quite interested to hear more about your profession. I, too, have enjoyed bird watching, although not on a professional scale."

Falk remained silent.

"Of course, we both know that is not what you really do." Abu Scha beckoned to one of the two women, and she came immediately to his side, bending forward to allow the man to whisper in her ear. Then she straightened, nodded, and left the room. The second woman remained. "We both know the importance of the meetings going on at the lighthouse and what it will mean when the three scientists exchange data, agree to work as a team and flesh out a common plan for the application of solar energy. You seem interested in my reason for being here. I see no harm in confirming for you it is to see that this plan does not remain the sole right of the three countries involved."

Falk could no longer stay silent. "What do you want from me?"

"Nothing, Mr. Falk. But then perhaps there is one small

thing." He leaned forward, the light from the table lamp next to him reflecting in his jet-black eyes. "I want to be sure you die like the rest of your people at the lighthouse. There must be, you see, no one left to tell what happened."

"If you know who I am, then you must also be aware there are other people than me involved in insuring the meeting is not in interfered with."

"Yet, you have suffered the loss of two security agents already. I would consider that interference, Mr. Falk."

"It was, and security has been increased."

Abu Scha leaned back in his chair. "You started with four security personal, including yourself. Two are dead, and you are here, leaving only two trained security agents at the lighthouse." Scha smiled. "You look confused, Mr. Falk. I'm counting the replacement who was also killed."

Falk churned inwardly at the man's smooth confidence.

"I hardly consider you being here, with only two people left to take care of the scientists, an 'increase in security'." As if an afterthought, Scha waved his hand nonchalantly. "And I understand one of the agents is a woman."

Falk now knew for certain he'd been correct in surmising there was a traitor in the lighthouse. There was no other way that Abu Scha could know such details. "I would advise your informer in the lighthouse," Falk replied, "to forget whatever it is you're planning as I can assure you it will not work out. Do you believe a meeting of such importance would not have multiple contingency arrangements?"

"Nice try, Mr. Falk. We will get what we came for and nothing you might have done will stop us." Abu Scha looked up as the woman came back into the room. "All set?" he asked.

"Yes. Mr. Falk's car is waiting. I gave his ticket to the valet parking attendant; there were no questions."

"Very good. You have everything packed?"

"Yes."

Falk cursed softly. They'd taken the parking stub when they'd cleaned him out. Now he was going for a ride in his own car.

"Hope you don't mind. My car is parked in the hotel garage, and there is a good possibility it is being watched. I don't wish to find out the hard way. As for your rental car, you will have no use for it after I arrive at my next destination. So, I strongly suggest you place yourself in the hands of of my two beautiful assistants. I will drive. You have only to sit back and enjoy the ride."

The Solar Triangle

Chapter 55

Koski heard the scraping of chairs in the meeting room and then voices all speaking at once. She didn't need to consult her wristwatch. It was after three in the morning; she'd had to leave her position at the door briefly to make the code exchange at three. Swale had not returned and now that the meeting was over, she could search for him. As the attendees filed out of the room, still talking, she noticed a different, more cheerful attitude, and prayed it meant things were almost wrapped up. Tanner and Courtney were the last out. The commander hadn't returned after his sudden departure. Swale's report that the man was resting in bed had made her feel a little better. She would ask his roommate, Professor Teesdale, to let her know that he was still safe in bed.

"Koski, don't you ever sleep?" Courtney asked as she stood beside Tanner in the doorway.

"I cat-nap every so often while you all are working."

"But not tonight, I see," Tanner intoned looking into her red-rimmed eyes. "I'm going up to the radio room. I need Falk down here. The meeting is as good as over. All we need is the commander's signature and it's all done. Finished."

Courtney smiled. "I never thought we'd do it. I was getting worried toward the end. Then the commander got sick and removed himself."

"It was a blessing," Tanner grunted. "We got more done with him out of the way than with his constant nit-picking."

"Going up to the radio room won't do any good, Mr. Tanner. Falk has his orders," Koski said with icy venom.

"We'll see about that," Tanner replied curtly.

"Let him go, Koski," Courtney said. "He has to get it out of his system. He'll yell and carry on through the door, that's all."

Koski was about to spit out a pithy retort when, searching her pocket, she suddenly realized she'd left the key in the door. "Damn," she said, pushing past Courtney, who stepped back in alarm. "I have to stop him!" Koski ran after Tanner, and, to her relief, saw him, as Courtney had said, standing at the door and yelling for Falk to let him in. Suddenly, Tanner saw the key and, without hesitation, turned it and pushed the door open. To his surprise, the room was empty.

He turned as Koski entered, a fierce frown on both their faces.

"What's going on here? Where is Falk? I thought…"

"Sit down, Mr. Tanner," she ordered, pointing to one of the chairs. "We have a lot to discuss."

Tanner's face had turned ashen by the time she finished explaining. "You mean Falk is on the mainland? There's just you and Swale for security?"

"Yeah, and I don't know where Swale is."

Tanner stared at her in disbelief. He opened and closed his mouth without speaking as she continued. "Falk wanted to call in the Navy. You countermanded his orders. He had do something. He couldn't communicate with the outside while here in the lighthouse. We were convinced all our communications were being intercepted."

"When will he be back, and what are his orders?"

"All I know is he should be back sometime tomorrow evening." She glanced at her watch. "Make that this evening."

Tanner stared at the radio equipment as if willing it to send out a call for help.

"I can transmit a mayday signal," she said softly.

"No, not yet. I need the commander's agreement first."

"Then we'd better go down and get it at once."

Tanner nodded and left the radio room followed by Koski who made sure she locked the door this time and kept the key.

The Solar Triangle

Chapter 56

Swale was relieved of his weapon and flashlight, then thoroughly searched. Hands lashed behind his back by plastic cords, he was tossed face down against a grassy hillock and ordered to remain silent. He watched out of the corner of one eye as his papers, illuminated by the beam of the industrial flashlight, were scrutinized.

"Blimey! This bloke's from MI-6!" A muffled conversation followed which Swale strained to hear. Finally, someone squatted beside him. "What are you doing here?"

Swale rolled over and squirmed to reposition a rock sticking in the middle of his back. "It's a long story. How long do you have?"

The SAS man leaned in close. "As long as it takes for you to tell me and for me to believe what you say. Start talking."

Swale revealed most of the truth about his general mission, leaving out some salient facts. The man grunted, reached into an inside pocket of his jump suit, and removed a card showing his name, rank, and serial number—stamped and dated by British Second Parachute Regiment and nothing else. "If we are captured, this is the only information we would give to the enemy." He indicated the man beside him. "His card is an American version of this one."

"I understand," Swale said softly.

"And the bit about the regiment isn't completely true." Swale caught a flash of white teeth as the man grinned.

"Are you holding the old Scotsman a prisoner?" Swale asked.

"We are. What is he to you?"

The rock pressed painfully in his back, and Swale grunted. "Hard to say. I think we spoiled his vacation. Where is he?"

"Out of the way for now," the man replied.

"What are you going to do with me?"

"You'll stay with us. Our job is to watch the outside of the lighthouse until we're told otherwise."

"I can show you a way in."

"Mr. Swale. We know the way in. And if we needed to, we could do so even if it were locked and bolted up. We do as ordered. We wait."

Chapter 57

The document Tanner thrust beneath the commander's nose brought the poor man to a startled awareness. The commander signed after some complaining, saying he was signing under duress. In fact, no one cared what he said as long as he signed off on the document. Once signed, it meant they could call the Navy to take them off the island. It also meant that each of the three mediators, Tanner, Courtney, and the commander would get a copy of the finished agreement, along with the written details laid down by the scientists for a working solar energy program. What Tanner didn't dare mention was that it included the plans for an enhanced Engine of Fire, capable of vaporizing anything focused on.

Tanner, looking flushed and triumphant, turned to Koski. "Okay, Agent Koski, send the message. Tell the Navy to come and get us."

Koski headed to the radio room, unlocked the door, and sat in front of the transmitter, flipped the on switch and prepared to make her call. A puff of smoke issued from the transmitter accompanied by an acrid odor Then, every piece of equipment in the room sizzled and arced. Horrified, Koski pulled open the drawer that Swale had shown her when he first introduced her to the radio room. The small box was still there, but the printed circuit board was gone. Someone had installed it into the transmitter, knowing it would self-destruct every piece of electrical equipment in the lighthouse and surrounding area. She pulled her cell phone from her pocket and switched it on. Nothing. It was exactly as Swale had said; there was no way anyone could send or receive a message. Glancing at the wall clock, she calculated it would be an hour and a quarter before the Navy transmitted their code exchange. How long would it be before they realized the problem and sent help? Koski slumped in the chair. She was the last remaining security agent. Falk wouldn't be back for hours. It was all up to her. The next second, she jumped to her feet, readying herself for the challenge. The first thing she needed to do was discover who had sabotaged the transmitter.

Chapter 58

Abu Scha spoke briefly with Ian McLean by cell phone then left the hotel with Falk. Now, as the first streaks of dawn clawed through the wintry sky, McLean called his men together. It was time to move out. The team was ready; they reassembled, then moved quickly and silently out of the hangar, carrying their packed equipment to an old, but superbly maintained three-ton-army truck. The engine kicked over at once. McLean nodded his satisfaction. This was the way he intended the entire operation to proceed.

The copter mechanic, in his small room at the back of the office, heard the truck's engine. The team was leaving, and that meant it was time for him to abandon the airstrip, but he had one more important job to carry out. When completed, he would close the five-barred gate, drive to the dock, and take the ferry back to Oban.

The truck bounced along the country road loaded with two deflated Zodiacs, an air pump generating system, ammunition, hard tack rations, water, and a two-way radio communications system that would enable McLean to keep in constant contact with his employer, Abu Scha. The truck drove three miles from the airstrip to a point on a lonely cliff-side road forty feet above the sea. The packages were lowered down the cliff face to a small, sandy cove. The team followed, rappelling down, quickly inflating the boats and loading them with ammunition, guns and supplies. It was still dark enough to shield them from sight as they push off the beach, rode the waves out to the open sea and headed for the Flangenan lighthouse.

Chapter 59

Falk sat in the back seat between the two demure-looking Middle Eastern women while Abu Scha drove through the pre-dawn darkness. Falk could see the dash clock glowing green, showing five fifty-five in the morning. They had been driving for over three hours, and Falk wondered when he would be missed. Whenever, it was enough to die.

Over the next hour, he watched the scenery with a practiced eye. A highway sign indicating they were travelling on the A82 flashed by, meaning they were travelling the main route between Glasgow and Fort William, a town in the southern Highlands.

Scha glanced at Falk in the rear view mirror. "Enjoying the ride, Mr. Falk? We're nearing Glencoe. An Historic place, I understand—the site of the infamous battle between the McDonald and Campbell clans. I study history because it fascinates, and at the same time, teaches me so much about humankind. The Scots, for example, were barbaric in their fighting prowess, yet at the same time they were worldclass poets. Take the name Glencoe. Translated, it means: 'The Vale of Weeping'."

The clock showed almost seven.

Glencoe, in the early morning hours, drenched by rain all seasons of the year, looked dramatic and menacing.

"Yeah, thanks for the guided tour, but how about a little relief from these damn restraints?"

Scha chuckled. "Don't worry, Mr. Falk, we don't have far to go now. You'll soon be out of your misery."

One of the women said something in Arabic. Scha nodded but said nothing. They drove in silence for fifteen more minutes, then turned off the highway onto a small, narrow road surrounded by trees and hedges so thick and overgrown that the sides of the car brushed against the thick foliage, all the time climbing higher into the hills. Scha stopped the car at a branch in the narrow lane; it was no longer wide enough to be called a road. An old wooden signpost leaned drunkenly at the Y, one finger pointing to Ballachulish, the words almost obliterated from years of coarse wind and rain barrelling down from the highlands. The other finger pointed westward indicating two miles to Clatch.

Scha swung the car in the direction of Clatch and drove a mile until they arrived at a wooden gate and what had once been a driveway, now an overgrown slash of gravel through the dense green grass. The woman on the nearside of the car opened her door, climbed out and walked to the gate. She tugged hard to get it open, pulling and lifting the heavy gate to allow clearance over the uneven ground. Falk had felt a rush of frigid air when the woman opened the car door, and knew if the temperature fell another degree or two it would begin to snow.

Scha drove through the gate and waited until it was shut before continuing up the driveway. "Once we arrive at the house, I'll see you get the restraints off, Mr. Falk. You will not be going anywhere. We could all use something warm to drink after our journey. I want to be sure you are well and in good health right up to the moment of my departure. You see, you are my insurance, my hostage. I have no doubt we have been, or will be, followed. I never underestimate my enemy. Now, if you were foolish enough to try an attempt to escape from this place, you would discover you had made a very serious mistake: If you step anywhere except this driveway, you'll find it all swampland. You would sink away in a matter of minutes. A dreadful way to die, I'm told."

Falk digested the threat. The area outside seemed to fit the description. Marshland, bog, swamp, quicksand, call it whatever, Falk was aware that there were certain areas in the southern Highlands that, for hundreds of years, had been swallowing man and beast, leaving no trace. He had no intention of becoming the next victim by running headlong into such an unfriendly environment.

Scha pulled up in front of a rundown farmhouse. One window was boarded up, and the front porch sagged alarmingly. One of the three wooden steps leading up to the entrance had no cross member. As Scha switched off the engine, the front door opened, the face of a weathered, bearded face staring through the opening. On seeing his Syrian employer, he opened the door wider revealing his shaggy, bent-shouldered frame. He looked to be in his eighties and was dressed in what had once been a blue serge suit, twenty-five years earlier. A woollen muffler was wrapped around his neck and stuffed down the front of his pants, covering the fact that he wore no shirt. On his feet were a pair of muddy green Wellington boots with his pant legs stuffed into them. Topping his natty attire, he sported a filthy, stained Glengarry cap, tilted at a rakish angle with one of the usual two black ribbon streamers missing. Stringy reddish-gray hair shot out at all angles from beneath the cap.

Abu Scha opened his door and called to the Scot. "Good morning, everything under control?"

"Aye, 'tis," the man replied, giving the evil eye to Falk.

"I want you to take good care of our guest," Scha announced. "He's my insurance policy until the plane arrives."

With a women on either side, Falk was escorted into the farmhouse behind Scha and the suited Scot.

Inside, the farmhouse was in better shape than it looked from outside. Falk decided it was being used for a safe house and remembered Swale mentioning the Irish Republican

Army had discovered it was far easier to move around in Scotland without being hounded by British troops than it was at home. The farmhouse was likely an IRA favorite "loaner,". and Abu Scha was probably one of many permitted to use the lonely place for an acceptable fee.

Falk did a quick assessment. To the casual passerby the place would look deserted, if they even noticed the place at all from the lane. A portable oil heater in the hallway and another in the kitchen were pouring out heat. Three table lamps in the room were oil fired. No electrical appliances meant no utility company to answer to. He had no doubt the same went for natural gas. As far as outside communication, they would rely solely on cell phones.

One of the women walked Falk to a kitchen chair and indicated he sit. The other woman, on Scha's orders, left to bring the car around to the back of the house. The ill-suited Scot went over to a butane-powered stove, removed from it a steaming brown teapot, brought it over to the table, and set it down. He jerked his thumb toward a cupboard. "Cups are in there." The women crossed the room, collected five cups and placed them on the table while the Scot removed a bottle of milk and a bag of sugar from another cupboard. Scha sat at the table across from Falk, silently watching the procedure. Noting Falk's eyes darting from one place to another, he offered, "As you can see, we are self-sufficient here." Smiling sardonically, he added, "All the comforts of home" as a cup of steaming tea was slid in front of Falk, who, with his hands still cuffed behind his back, was unable to reach it.

Scha said a few words in Arabic and Falk's right hand was released, while the other hand was affixed to the back of the chair.

"You said I'd be released from these when we arrived," Falk complained.

"And you will; however, for now, just one hand. Enjoy your tea."

It was obvious Falk would not be given the chance to make any moves detrimental to Abu Scha's departure. Falk sipped his tea as the three Arabs engaged in conversation in their native tongue. The Scot left the room, leaving the four of them at the kitchen table. *Where would Scha's plane land if what he had said about marshland and swamps were true?* Falk wondered. Was the warning earlier a ploy to make him believe that any attempt to escape would be hopeless? With his free hand, Falk slicked back a strand of chestnut hair that had fallen forward as thoughts continued to run through his mind.

The back door of the kitchen opened, and a cold blast of air rushed into the room ahead of a huge, brindle-colored mastiff, held at the end of a chain by the Scotsman. The animal lunged toward the group at the table with a lusty growl.

The chain brought the dog up short, although the large-as-a-boar monster continued tugging forward as if wanting to sink its fangs into the closest throat.

"Down ye bloody heathen! Get down!" The man thrust one of his green rubber boots into the beast's ribs, and the dog slowly obeyed, though its eyes glared at the newcomers with obvious hostility. "It'll nay harm ye as long as I've hold of him." Falk silently hoped the man had a good grip.

Abu Scha had remained calm throughout the entire entrance of man and beast. "I am sure you will take good care of the animal, but there is no need for concern," he said, indicating with a flick of his hand one of the women. "She can speak to animals, they understand her." The dog turned its head toward Scha and growled a rumbling, thunder-in-the-distance sound as if issuing a defiant challenge.

The woman pushed back her chair, stood, pointed at the dog, and at the same time began making strange guttural sounds as she walked toward the animal. At once the dog sat up straight, ears twitching, eyes staring blankly straight ahead as the sounds, now resonating a tone deeper, began undulating like the sound of wind through cut bamboo. Reaching forward, she rested her hand on the dog's head. The animal never moved, and Falk was amazed to see the dog's eyes begin to lower until it was sitting motionless, its eyes closed; slowly sinking from a sitting position to lay on its side as if asleep. Kneeling, the woman leaned over and murmured into the dog's left ear, while slowly rubbing and stroking its head. It was as if the dog was in a deep sleep.

The old man, his mouth agape, stood holding the now slackened chain. "Witchcraft! Bloody witchcraft! I've owned that dog for eight years, since it were born, and never have I seen anything like this. He's na dead, is he?"

"No," the woman replied, to his surprise, in perfect English. "He will sleep until I allow him to awaken. And when he does, he and I will be the best of friends."

"It's still witchcraft, woman, and I dinna care for such things," the Scot growled. "Wake up my dog!"

"The dog will remain asleep until after I leave," Abu Scha hissed. "Why did you bring the beast in here in the first place?"

"I was going to feed it."

"Then it can wait until after we leave." As Scha sipped his tea, Falk glimpsed the dial of the man's watch. It was nine in the morning. Unless Stewart's man could locate him, and soon, he was going to have to escape. The odds for either, however, didn't look good.

Chapter 60

Koski quickly exited the radio room. The acrid smoke from within quickly dissipated. A quick look about informed her there were no flames. Locking the door behind her, she decided to remain silent about the equipment. There were only two people who knew what had occurred; she and the person who had sabotaged the electronics.

"Agent Koski."

She jumped at the sound of her name. Looking nervously in the direction of the voice, she saw Doctor Jenner. "I have to talk with you!" he said, approaching. He looked as if he'd not slept for days. For a moment, she had the awful feeling that the smell from the smoke was still clinging to her clothing and he would glean what had happened.

"Yes, Doctor, what is it?"

"Now that the meeting is over and plans exchanged, I am concerned about the safety of the documents. You are the only security agent I can find. What happened to Falk and Swale?"

Koski stood straighter and flashed her eyes at him with confidence, knowing she would have to choose her next words with care. "Agent Swale is on outside perimeter patrol, and Agent Falk is in the radio room on special assignment. I assure you there's no need for alarm."

"If I didn't know better, I would believe you. You're good at your job."

Koski said nothing, her body remaining alert and at attention, although her mind was racing ahead. What did the man mean?

Jenner continued. "I was near the radio room a few minutes ago just as you were leaving, and Agent Falk was not in the room. There was smoke in the room. I recognized the fumes from an electrical fire. What happened?"

It was clear to Koski it was time to come clean: Tanner knew and perhaps Doctor Jenner should learn the reality of their situation. There was a traitor afoot. But was Jenner really trying to find out the truth, or was he covering up his own traitorous actions? Betting on the first, she revealed the facts of their dilemma and the importance of remaining silent, stressing that he not pass the information on to the others.

"I understand the gravity of our situation, but I do not agree with remaining silent. It would be more to our benefit to advise everyone where things stand. That way we can prepare for the worst while hoping for the best."

Koski squared her shoulders. The man was right. She wondered briefly what Falk might have done under the same circumstances, but Falk wasn't there. He'd had abandoned her. As hard as the decisions facing her were, she relished the power to make them for herself.

It was as if Jenner was reading her mind. "It seems to me we should make a stand here in the lighthouse until the authorities come to get us. You do realize that under these conditions, and with the accumulated knowledge we have exchanged, we are an invaluable prize to whatever country can seize the moment before we can be evacuated safely off of this godforsaken place?"

"Of course, I know. That's why I was assigned here in the first place." Koski snapped back. Privately, her thinking already adjusted to the new circumstances. She now believed as Jenner had said, that everyone would have to be told. There was nothing to lose. The traitor or traitors in their midst would remain silent. It would be up to her to watch for the slightest sign that would give him, her or them away. To Jenner, she decreed, "I'll inform the group of our current condition."

The Solar Triangle

Chapter 61

"What's wrong with them?" Dr. Kevin Clayton asked as he sat in the kitchen next to Courtney Spencer. Jack Tanner and the commander were huddled together at table across the room.

Spencer studied Tanner over the rim of her cup. "Wrong?"

"I thought they'd be over the moon now that our work is done. All we have to do now is wait for the Navy to haul us back to the mainland. Tanner seems to be in a decidedly worse mood than I would have expected," Clayton complained.

Tanner glanced toward the couple, said a few words to the commander, pushed back his chair and headed in their direction.

"Perhaps he's going to tell us," Spencer said. Before Tanner could say anything, she spoke. "I see the commander is up and around. Feeling better, is he?"

"Improving, though not fully recovered, I can assure you." Without waiting for a response, he continued. "Agent Koski wants to update us on the current situation. We're to gather in the meeting room this morning at nine."

Clayton checked his watch. "Situation? What does that mean?"

"I think it better if we let her inform us, Doctor. I have to tell the others. Excuse me," Tanner said. He strode across the room, said a couple of words to the commander, and left.

"Do you know anything about a 'situation,' Courtney?" Clayton asked.

"I'm no wiser than you. I'll go and find Doctor Jenner. See you in the meeting room in ten minutes."

For Doctor Kevin Clayton the last few days at the light-house had been the most difficult of his entire career. Not only had working out the plans been harrowing in its technical aspects, but the constant injection of bureaucratic minutiae combined with the abrasive relations between the commander and Tanner, on top of the murder of two security agents by a yet unknown assassin, had made it a minor miracle the three scientists had completed their task. He had not mentioned the conversation he'd had with Swale to anyone. He had a feeling they were about to hear more from Agent Koski about a 'situation' that had gone from bad to worse.

Chapter 62

Swale and Jock were being held together in a freshly dug slit trench cunningly camouflaged in a rocky hillside within sight of the lighthouse. Their two SAS guards were watching them closely. Swale observed one of two spin the dials on his compact radio communicator. Something was wrong. The radio operator slapped the side of the radio. "Damn thing's not working. It's dead."

The second soldier, studying the lighthouse through a pair of high-powered binoculars, continued his vigil and said, "Check the circuit breaker; these radios never quit."

"First thing I did. It's fine. I'm telling you, we're off the air."

"Here, let me check it. You keep an eye on the lighthouse and these two."

The two men swapped positions. The second soldier got the same result. Swale saw the man was puzzled. "It's the first time I've seen this model go on the fritz. I'll try my personal." The soldier removed a cell-like phone from his pack and spoke rapidly. It was apparent to Swale, it too was off the air. There could only be one explanation: Someone had installed the self-destruct module and taken out the communications in the lighthouse along with all other electronic transmitting-receiving devices within a thirty-mile radius.

"One of you needs to go get the NCO in charge," Swale said softly. "I have some bad news for him."

The soldier shot him back a fast look. "Keep quiet, mate. You might be a big-shot MI-6 agent, but until we've done our job, you are about as important as that old guy next to you."

Jock, who seemed asleep, opened an eye and glared at the soldier. "Young heathen! Ye should respect yer elders. If this man says he has something to say, I'd make certain someone hears him oot."

The man with the binoculars looked back over his shoulder. "I suppose we'd better tell the boss. We can't stay out of communication."

He'd no sooner finished talking when, seemingly out of nowhere, a figure slid into the trench. It was the sergeant in charge of the six-man team. "We're off the air," he muttered.

"I know. One of us was getting ready to get over to you. What happened?"

"Dunno yet. We'll stay in our positions and watch the lighthouse. If anything happens, I'll give the signal—three blasts on my whistle—and we move out and take them as planned."

"If you would allow me to say something, Sergeant, I

may be able to save you a lot of trouble. If your mission is to look after the occupants of the lighthouse, you should know that my friend here used to be the lighthouse keeper. He's lived in the place most of his life. We can get you inside with no problem."

"If you mean the pipe, we know about that," the sergeant answered. "Our job is two-fold: If any attack is made on the place, we take out the attackers and nab at least a couple alive to hand over to the authorities for a full interrogation. However, as long as there is no actual attack, we are to presume the lighthouse occupants are safe and only observe. The Royal Navy will be notified directly by those inside the lighthouse."

"Not any more, Sergeant. Like your team has pointed out, there is no communication at the lighthouse."

The sergeant's face darkened, and Swale waved his hand. "Here's what happened."

When Swale finished, the wiry NCO rubbed his chin thoughtfully. "And this old guy knows all about running a lighthouse, right? I mean the old fashioned way?"

Jock leaned forward. "Of course I know how to run a light the auld fashioned way. A mon never forgets."

"Good. You might just get the chance to prove it, Grandpa."

The Solar Triangle

Chapter 63

McLean's plan was working perfectly. The two Zodiacs were at sea, two miles behind the fishing boats that had sailed from Tiree before dawn. McLean was aware the fishing boats would show up on the Navy's radar. The Zodiacs, small and hidden amidst the reflected signals from the fishing fleet, would be invisible. They would remain inside the protective cone, being sure to avoid any visual sighting by the fishermen, who would be busy preparing their nets and equipment. As the fishing fleet proceeded past Flangenan Island, the Zodiacs would drop back along the southeastern shore and land in a small, sandy cove. The location had been chosen for its remoteness and ideal natural cover, the two allowing McLean's men to approach from a direction that made it impossible for anyone guarding the lighthouse to observe.

As the boats wallowed slowly through the waves, McLean felt the excitement rise within him. The sea was running just under two feet high, an ideal height to lessen the chance of being sighted as they made their move toward the island. McLean throttled the outboard down, causing the craft to slow until he could feel the current pulling him closer to the island. He and his team, some of them men who had sailed these waters for years, had studied seasonal charts and tide reports until they could recite facts in their sleep. They knew the importance of making their landing unobserved and the attack successful. If so, each man would be rich for the rest of his life.

Fifteen minutes later, McLean increased the throttle and surged the boat ahead. Swinging his arm high over his head, he pointed to port, giving the signal to the following vessel, which immediately followed the graceful arc of the wake ahead of him.

Chapter 64

"Ma dog's been asleep for almost two hours, missus. He's never slept that long during the day. If he dies…"

"Your animal is in a deep sleep. He will not die," the Middle Eastern woman assured him, adjusting her head scarf.

The ancient Scot, stiff with anger. turned to Abu Scha. "Ma job was to see you safe until you were collected at the agreed spot. It dinna include her," he pointed an accusing finger at the woman, "casting a spell on ma dog."

Scha had no time to waste. "You're being paid. The dog is fine. Don't bother me with such things." Unfortunately, his words didn't seem to calm the man.

"This is Scotland and I dinna care how much you're paying me. We take care of our animals here. We dinna eat our dogs."

Scha's face reddened at the racial slur. He'd never allowed anyone to speak to him this way and remain alive, but he needed the man to get him to the rendezvous point for his flight to Norway. Swallowing his pride, Abu Scha turned to the woman who had put the dog to sleep. "Wake the brute. Show this fool his dog is fine."

The woman crossed the room and knelt beside the

hound. Pressing behind the animal's left ear, she again made the deep throaty sound and the mastiff's hind left leg twitched. Then the dog gave a deep sigh, sat up, and shook itself as if it had just come in from a heavy rain. The woman straightened, smiled at the Scot, and returned to her chair in the kitchen.

The old man approached the dog, but the animal bared its teeth and growled as if the Scot were a stranger. Then it turned, trotted across the room and sat at the woman's feet.

Falk watched the performance in awe. He had never before seen a dog hypnotized, if that was, in fact, what the woman had done.

"I see you are impressed, Mr. Falk. There are many things in my country that are not widely known to the Western world."

"I'm sure there are, Mr. Scha. There are also things here in Scotland of which even you may not be aware."

Ignoring Falk's remark, Scha watched the Scotsman glare across the room at his dog. The man was quivering with anger. Suddenly, he turned and walked out of the house, slamming the door shut behind him. Falk was right. One thing Scha and the Arabic woman couldn't appreciate was how dangerous an enemy they had just created.

Concerned for his own safety, Scha gave a quick nod to the woman with the dog at her feet, indicating she should follow and watch the Scotsman. As she rose, the mastiff jumped to its feet and followed, the door clattering shut behind them.

For a moment, silence filled the small room. Then the unmistakable roar of a shotgun came from outside, followed by a second blast. The remaining woman was on her feet and out the door with startling suddenness. Scha ran to the window and pulled back a sacking-like curtain. What he saw caused him to back away and remove a 9 mm Sig Sauer from his shoulder holster.

A woman's scream and the braying of the mastiff hit Falk and Scha's ears together in a cacophony of fear and rage.

Then the unforgettable, ugly signature of a shotgun being cocked sounded outside in the frosty air. Scha's face contorted with fear as he raced toward the unlocked door, his automatic pointing forward. As he approached, the shotgun roared and the wooden door splintered apart in a gush of orange flame, flinging Scha back amid a hail of shattering lead shot whose force spun and turned him several times before he hit the propane stove and slithered in a bloody mass to the floor.

Falk, still attached by one hand to the back of his chair, stared in disbelief at the blood-spattered Scot, swaying in the shattered door frame. Behind the man, he could see a woman, lying on the ground beside the dog. Both were dead. As the old man turned to leave, Falk saw the bone handle of a knife sticking from between his shoulder blades. The Scot never uttered a word as he fell forward, his mission completed.

Half-standing, Falk lifted, then smashed the chair against the edge of the table until he was free of the wrist re-straint, then, with the plastic manacle dangling from his wrist, walked outside to view the carnage. The dog-controlling woman was crumpled in a bloody heap at the side of the car, her body shattered by the first blast from the shotgun. Not only had she been killed, but the shot had wiped out the front end of the car and blown one of the front tires to shreds. The dog was lying beside her. The second woman, was lying flat on her back a few feet from the old man. She was without a face, her head scarf only partially hiding the damage. In a matter of minutes, four people had been killed by one man's blind rage. No premeditation. All had met their death over a dog.

The car was useless. Falk would have to make it on foot to the nearest town to contact Stewart and convey what had happened. It was midmorning, and an already dark sky was filling with heavy clouds. The freezing air smelled of snow.

Returning back into the farmhouse, Falk searched through the carry-on bag that Abu Scha had carried with him from the hotel. It contained a large amount of cash in sterling, several books of traveller's checks, three different passports, and a 9 mm Beretta 3R with a 15-round magazine in place and another spare in the bottom of the bag. Falk hefted the weapon, feeling the balance of its 2.47-pound weight, and stuck it into his jacket pocket along with the spare clip.

Thinking back to his car ride, he recalled a signpost pointing to a town with an odd name. What was it? It was alongside the road near where they had turned to the farm. Clatch! That was the name. At least now he knew where he was going. The sign had read two miles, and they had travelled half a mile before they turned into the remote farm house's gravel driveway. He could make the walk with no problem, but first he had to do something about the damned wrist restraint.

He quickly sifted through several sideboard drawers, coming at last across a hefty kitchen knife. Shoving back the sleeve of his jacket, he worked the knife back and forth under the thick plastic until eventually it gave way. He was free.

He left the scene of carnage without a backward glance, knowing that, once contacted, Stewart would send a clean-up crew and no one would ever be the wiser.

The Solar Triangle

Chapter 65

Koski, standing at the head of the table in the meeting room, watched the various inhabitants react to her announcement.

Jenner was the first to speak. "You're telling us that we may have to defend ourselves against a possible terrorist attack. Am I correct?"

"Yes, Doctor, at least until the Navy gets no response from an attempted code exchange. Then they will proceed here at once."

"When is the next exchange due?" Tanner asked.

Koski looked at her watch and replied, "One and a half hours from now," adding, "and I advise we secure the lighthouse in the meantime."

"I agree with Agent Koski," Clayon offered. "We could be attacked at any moment, and by the time the Navy realizes something is wrong, they could be too late."

Koski stood with her arms braced against the table and looked at into the grim faces around her, wondering which one was the face of the traitor. Would he or she make a move? Do something—anything—that would enable her to recognize and take him or her out?

Koski knew there would be no mercy shown once they were attacked. She had to be ready, no matter what it took to protect these people and stop the documents from the meeting falling into adversarial hands. Swale had not returned. Falk was not due back for several more hours. The thought that she might never see Falk again sent a shiver down her spine, at the same time, reinforcing her determination to defend the lighthouse, its occupants and the meeting documents at all costs.

"Agent Koski is correct. We must prepare for the worst," the commander snapped in his usual bombastic manner. "Having served in leadership positions in The Royal Navy in various skirmishes around the world, I will be happy to take command until such time as the Navy arrives."

Tanner immediately reacted to commander's words like a bull to a waving red flag. "Who made you the leader? There are others here who have equal ability to lead."

"I, too, would be happy to donate any military advice I can," Professor Teesdale quavered. "I served with the LDV— the Home Guard Local Defense Volunteers—during the war. We trained once a week and patrolled our village in case of invasion. We were going to be issued rifles, but they never arrived, so we drilled with broomsticks…"

Kevin Clayton and Courtney Spencer exchanged smiles at the old man's enthusiastic offer.

"Thank you, Professor. I'm sure when the time comes, you will be a most useful member of the team," Koski replied. Teesdale's face lit up with joy at her positive words.

"I'm sorry, everyone, but as the sole remaining security agent in a time of emergency, you will have to take orders from me. Those were my instructions, agreed upon by our governments, and I'm afraid that's the way it's going to be," Koski stated. Not wanting any arguments, she continued. "There are one or two things I want you to see. Follow me."

She led the group to the spot where beneath the carpet the trapdoor led to the room below and pipe exit. "Beneath this carpet, a small room leads to a large pipe which extends out to the sea. It is possible to walk through the pipe to the outside without any trouble." She looked hard at her group. "It is also possible that whoever might attack the lighthouse is also aware of the conduit. They may decide to use it as a means of entry or a way to kill us one by one if using it to escape. It must therefore remain under constant guard until the threat of invasion has passed."

With the assistance of the group, she pulled back the carpet and lifted the trapdoor. Everyone gathered around the hole as she shined her flashlight beam down into the room. Looking back at everyone, she volunteered, "The rest of the story is that we discovered a man living in that room and took him into custody."

"My God!" Tanner exploded. "Who was it? Where is he?" Slowly, Koski straightened to a standing position. She knew what she was about to disclose would not go over well. "We will have to await the return of Agent Swale. You see, he was checking on the man prior to his patrol around the island."

"You mean you had an unknown person living down there all the time we were holding our meeting?" The commander's voice shifted to alto as he uttered the words.

"The meeting was at no time in any danger from him. He's an old Scotsman who had come onto the island before the meetings started. The lighthouse was once his home. Each year he comes back to spend a few days. This time, however, he found his lighthouse being prepared for the meeting, so he went underground."

"Why didn't he leave when he saw the preparations going on? Surely he knew he would be in trouble if caught."

"He had been dropped off by a friend, a fisherman who left him, saying he would return in a few days. It was a ritual they had been doing for years. Sadly, once security tightened, his friend couldn't return to take him back."

"Couldn't he have been the one who killed two of our party and even now have killed Swale? He might be loose out there waiting to lead whoever is planning to attack us in through the pipe or kill us if we try to escape?" Spencer asked. Koski detected a different feeling between them. They were was no longer on congenial woman-to-woman terms.

"Look," replied Koski. "Agent Falk made it quite clear to Mr. Tanner that, in his opinion, the meetings should've been scrubbed awhile ago. He was turned down in no uncertain terms." She glared at the group. "It was then he took it upon himself to go to the mainland in the hope of saving this operation. As it now stands, we may have lost Swale and Falk as well due to the stubborn refusal to cancel the meetings. All we can do at this point is work together to reorganize this place into a strong defensive position. To start with, we should work in pairs for safety. Commander Harris, Professor Teesdale and Mr. Tanner as one group, with Doctor Clayton, Ms. Spencer and Doctor Jenner another. At least this way, you will each be teamed together nationally. But remember, there can only be one of us in charge. This is no time for bruised egos. Do I make myself clear?" Koski asked.

A half-hearted murmur was the only reply.

"Okay. Here's what I have in mind to do," Koski said.

The Solar Triangle

Chapter 66

While everyone was grouped around Koski, Jenner's mind drifted back to an experience he'd had as a small Palestinian boy during the days of the struggle to create Israel. He had been eight years old.

His mother, father and sister, Rachel, aged three, along with him, aged six, arrived in Jaffa after a long and arduous trek from the crowded transit camps in Villach, Austria. His father, a noted Polish scientist, found work as a part-time photographer for a local newspaper. They lived in a small apartment, eking out a living like thousands of other displaced families.

One day, his father was assigned to cover three British soldiers found hanging by their necks in an orange grove on the outskirts of Jaffa. Little Jacob had begged his father to let him accompany him. As his father's assistant, he could carry some of the heavy equipment that photographers were burdened with in those days. His father had reluctantly agreed, justifying it to his wife by explaining that it was time the boy learned how difficult life in the new country could be. Upon their arrival, the grove was already filled with British troops, new people, even Movietone News was there to record the horrors of terrorist activities being waged in the small country: Arabs against Jews with the British trying to mediate a peace that for sixty-five years had not yet come into being. Jenner's father had told him simply that the soldiers had been captured and hanged.

Jenner watched as the press moved in closer to three trees from each of which a man hung from the branches. It was hot. The sun was directly overhead as ladders were placed against the trees. A British soldier climbed up each ladder to cut the rope and retrieve the body. Jacob complained to his father that it was so hot, he was feeling sick. His father, fearing the sight too overwhelming for his son, told him to sit beneath some large trees at the edge of the grove. His father would collect him after he'd taken pictures of the men being lowered to the ground. Jacob Jenner gladly followed his father's orders and sat, watching the activity, from the shade in a more detached manner from a hundred feet away.

The soldiers drew their knives to cut through the ropes. The media hushed and clustered closer as the soldier on the right severed a rope. What happened next would be forever imprinted on Jenner's mind. A bright orange flash and the entire area around the trees erupted in a gush of flame. Chunks of earth and pieces of bodies were flung into the bright blue sky. Stones and clumps of flaming grass thudded down about

Jacob to the screams of the injured and the dreadful odor of burning gunpowder and flesh. The area surrounding the three trees had been booby-trapped, and cutting the rope had set off a string of pre-wired land mines hidden in the earth beneath the feet of the onlookers and officials who had come to convey to the world the horrors of terrorism.

Jenner's father had died that day. One second he had been trying to earn a living, the next he was gone. Vaporized. Jenner had never forgotten or forgiven the Jewish terrorists who had carried out such an atrocious act against humankind. There had been other Jews among the now missing; it had made no difference to the terrorists. As Jenner grew into manhood and proceeded to become the renowned solar scientist, he carried with him a burning hatred against those who had killed his father on that day so long ago. Jenner never forgave Israel. He withdrew into himself and trusted no one. Now he was being asked to team up with an Israeli scientist and Ms. Courtney Spencer from the Mossad, and to put his trust in an agent whose nation was a dedicated friend of Israel.

A loud complaint from the commander brought him back to the real world.

"I must say, I don't consider it wise to lock ourselves inside the lighthouse. If attacked, we'll be sitting ducks. I suggest we disperse outside. Hide among the rocks until the

Royal Navy arrives. That way we'll have mobility and be harder to find."

"Commander, if you wish to go outside, please feel free to do so. I intend to seal and fortify this building against possible attack." Koski rechecked her watch. "In a very short while, the Navy will know we have a problem when they get no response from the code check. But until there's a rescue party outside the lighthouse, the main door and all windows will remain closed and blocked. We have enough water and supplies to last until they arrive." It was still early afternoon, and Jenner knew a look of determination when he saw one: Koski was determined to deliver them into the care of the Royal Navy no matter what.

Chapter 67

"Well, looks as if our cushy duty is over, Bob," a young navy radio operator said, leaning forward in his chair. "I was getting tired of sailing in circles and exchanging code numbers. Flag's message just now finally ends the exercise. Apparently everything's been completed faster than they expected."

"'About time, if you ask me. I mean, how many times do we have to retest our communications systems?" asked Bob.

"Our tax dollars at work. Hey! We'll be sailing in a straight line for the first time in days. Holy Loch, here we come."

The message from Flag at the Admiralty, London, to the Royal Navy vessels on watch off the coast of Flangenan had been simple and straightforward: *Operation Watchful complete. Return to base.* The same message was received by high-ranking officials in London, Tel-Aviv and Washington, D.C.

The Solar Triangle

Chapter 68

An unheard, collective sigh of relief issued from those who were waiting to hear that their scientist was ready to return home. Perhaps the happiest of all was the director of the Renewable Energy Program at the Weitzman Institute of Science in Rehovet, Israel.

Doctor Harry Levin had sighed alone in his office when he received word that the meetings were finished and Dr. Jacob Jenner would soon be on his way back to the Institute; the Royal Navy had apparently completed its task of guarding the meeting and was already streaming back to base in Scotland. Levin had slept very little since Jenner left Israel for the three-nation meeting. Levin had been against the conference from the start, and when the Israeli security man, Mordici Bern, had been discovered with his throat cut even before the meeting had started, he had complained vociferously to the Prime Minister, accusing him of endangering the future of Israel by allowing Dr. Jenner to leave the country.

Within minutes of his objection, Levin had been visited by two men in black who swore him to secrecy under threat of death and informed him why the government wanted Jenner to take part in the three-nation meeting.

Jenner, it seems, was the most valuable human to be employed by the Israeli government and its secret arm, the Mossad, to help fortify Israel's forces to ensure the nation's survival. What he would learn and bring back from the meeting would free Israel forever from the constant bloody fights for its existence. His contribution to the weapon was purposely flawed, but in such a discrete manner it would be months, perhaps years before the other two nations would discover the problem. Israel in the meantime would use their third of the plan and all the resources of the Institute and military to forge ahead and perfect a militarized version of the Engine of Fire with the ability to wipe out any city on earth in a matter of seconds. *And Shadrach, Meshach, and Abednego fell down bound into the midst of the burning fiery furnace.* Levin, of course, had felt a deep sadness when he heard this. Had it finally come to this? Israel would create a device capable of vaporizing hundreds of millions at a time. What the Mossad had not mentioned was, at that same meeting there was someone else present intending to do the exact same thing. Israeli intelligence had collected extensive information before allowing Jenner to go to the meeting and serve also as bait to catch that someone, and Levin was to remain privy to none of it.

Chapter 69

Halfway around the world, Tom Stewart held a copy of the Mossad dossiers on his desk. Their first reading had been most enlightening. He arranged them on his desk, one beside the other, in an attempt to order them by importance.

COMMANDER HAROLD HARRIS. JACK TANNER. COURTNEY SPENCER. DOCTOR KEVIN CLAYTON. PROFESSOR VICTOR TEESDALE. AGENT TIMOTHY SWALE.

Stewart had already reread the files on Commander Harris and Jack Tanner. Now he reached for the Courtney Spencer file, glancing at his watch as he reopened to the first page.

Fifty-five minutes later, he closed the dossier, leaned back in his chair, entwined his fingers and made a steeple out of both index fingers. Placing the point of the steeple beneath his chin, he nodded thoughtfully. *Cerberus* was always amassing, collating and interpreting vital information from all over the globe. In retrospect, he was now certain that he had been correct in assigning Falk and Koski to the scientific conference. If all went well, America, by right of its close association with Great Britain, could collect far more than just two-thirds of the plans for an advanced solar energy device. Once America's vast military-industrial complex was marshalled, the result would, without a doubt, be the most important addition to its arsenal of weapons since the conception of the atomic bomb.

America would, for the first time in history, be positioned to strike a truly surgical blow against organized terrorist groups, even perhaps organized crime in general, on the continental United States.

Leaning forward, he opened the Courtney Spencer file, turned to page thirty-two, and reread yet again the second paragraph from the top.

Spencer arrived in Israel at the age of twenty-four, having left her home in Boston after an argument with her parents, both Orthodox Jews. The reason for leaving has never been confirmed, although there are unsubstantiated reports it might have been due to an argument over a non-Jewish boyfriend she had wanted to marry. Her administrative skills were soon discovered, and she rose quickly in various departments of the Knesset, where she became Assistant to the Deputy Minister for Foreign Affairs. It is believed at that time she became a member of the Mossad's 'Black' section, although as expected, there is no actual evidence or hard copy files to prove or disprove this.

Tom Stewart was delighted with the information. He

would have been even more pleased if he could have gotten some feedback on Abu Scha from Falk. At present, he didn't even know Falk's whereabouts. Not reporting in usually indicated the situation was critical, and phoning him could cost his best agent his life. Instead, he reached for a phone and put a call through on the *Cerberu*s satellite to a contact in Oban.

The Solar Triangle

Chapter 70

It had started to snow by the time Falk was making his way down the narrow overgrown gravel road toward the lane they had turned from a few hours earlier. He'd searched the outbuildings in the hope of finding some kind of transportation, but found nothing.

Already, the top rail of the gate had gathered a half an inch of snow. He pried it open and squeezed through. Glancing back up the driveway, he noted his footprints already vanishing beneath the fresh snowfall. Turning up the collar of his jacket, he started walking toward the signpost that would lead him to Clatch. Once in Clatch, he could contact Stewart and arrange a fast pickup.

Falk had been walking twenty minutes when he heard the sound of an engine and looked back over his shoulder. Rumbling towards him, he saw a red tractor, moving about ten miles per hour, its huge tires splaying the newly fallen snow aside. The driver, sitting high above the road, must have seen Falk looking hopefully at him. The snow was falling faster now, and the driver had to squint against swirling flakes to make out the figure of a man standing in the middle of the road. He stopped and called down to Falk. "Where are ye going in this weather, man?"

"Clatch," Falk replied. "Car broke down."

"Climb up and hold on," the driver called. "I canna go fast, but I'm faster than walking." He re-engaged the gears, the roar of the engine removing any chance of questions or conversation, which was fine with Falk. Right now he was hoping for a store in town that sold warm jackets.

Arriving in Clatch, the driver slowed his tractor and stopped. "Here ye go. They have a public phone in the pub." He pointed to a group of buildings, one with a swinging sign proclaiming, "The Bonnie Prince."

Falk climbed down and thanked the man, who waved back and set off in a cloud of smoke and snow, and slowly vanished from sight.

Warmth hit him like a hot brick wall, the moment he walked through the door of The Bonnie Prince. A roaring coal fire filled the grate in the fireplace of the public room. There were two others in the room, seated at a small round table near the fire. Both old men stopped talking the moment Falk entered. They offered no words, but gave him a nod of greeting as he walked to the bar. The publican behind the polished redwood bar was drying a glass, which he set aside. "You look like ye could use a dram, sir."

"Please," Falk replied. The barman nodded and quickly had the drink on the bar. Falk took a long drink and sighed.

"Is there a phone I can use?"

"Over there, just around the corner on the wall."

Falk took another swallow of the fiery whisky, started for the phone, then stopped in mid-stride. Scha and his ladies had cleaned him out back at the hotel, and through long habit, he'd not taken with him any of the cash from Scha's tote bag. Falk knew to not to touch contraband money.

The barman asked, "Something wrong, sir?"

Falk walked back to the bar. "I don't have any money with me," he whispered.

Both men stared at each other, then Falk continued. "I wonder if you would make a phone call for me. The person on the other end will vouch for me."

"And who exactly might that be?"

"Someone in the government," Falk replied.

The bartender leaned forward and took a hard look at Falk. "And whose government would that be, then?"

"The American government."

"I see. Ye riding into town in a snowstorm on the top of tractor without coat, hat, or any other means of keeping warm. Ye walk in here, order a whisky, then tell me ye haven't the money to make a phone call to America, but that the American government will gladly pay?"

"How did you know I came on a tractor?"

The man nodded at a window with a clear view of the

spot where he'd dismounted. "We don't miss much in a small town like this."

"If I told you I was robbed by three Middle Easterners, would that help?"

"I doubt it, but go on."

"First, make the call to Oban. Then if you trust my government to pay for the call and my drink when they come to get me, I'll tell you the entire story."

"Oban, is it? Well, that I'll do. I would na put a long distance call through to Washington however."

"Fine, I appreciate it."

The publican reached under the counter and placed a battered black phone on the bar. "What's the number and ho do I ask for?"

Falk rattled off the number from memory. "Tell who ever answers that my name is Joe Falk and I work with Tom Stewart."

After a few words, the publican, satisfied that Falk was good for the drink and anything else he might need, handed the phone to Falk. Assured that a British Coast Guard helicopter would soon be on its way and would be landing in a space at the edge of town next to the historical marker within twenty minutes, he began to relax.

"Have a drink on the house, Mr. Falk, and now you can tell me about the three Arabs who robbed you."

Falk gladly accepted the drink, saying, "Two women and a man actually." After taking a sip of what proved to be an outstanding Scotch, he began his story. Twenty minutes later the thwacking rotor blades of a low flying helicopter thundered overhead, and the publican called to his wife. "Lorna, take over, I'm going to escort Mr. Falk to the monument."

The publican's Land Rover had him there before the copter landed.

Above, the copter lowered amid a flying swirl of snow to settle gently on the snow-covered turf. A door opened and a man bundled in a green flying suit jumped to the ground. He hurried over to them carrying another flying suit over his arm, and yelled at Falk over the roar of the engines, "Thought you might need this," and handed it to Falk, along with an envelope for the barman. "Thank you, sir, appreciate your help. This is for payment for Mr. Falk's bar bill and the phone call."

"Thanks for the hospitality," Falk offered as he struggled into the flight suit.

"Thanks for the story. It was a pip," the publican replied with a smile.

Falk and the airman ran to the craft and climbed aboard as it lifted off. Looking down, Falk waved goodbye and the publican waved back. Had the man believed his story about being robbed by three Arabs in an Indian restaurant in Glasgow, then being hijacked in his own car and dropped off in the Highlands? Falk hoped so. He'd been careful not to mentioned the house in the bog or the old Scot with the mastiff. Steward would clean up that mess in a hurry, so there'd be nothing to alert the media.

The co-pilot indicated a pair of earphones and pointed to his head. Falk nodded and slipped them on. "Here's the drill, Mr. Falk. We are going to fly you to Tiree and put you down at the airstrip. Constable Slat will meet you." The helicopter dipped and rolled through wind and snow. "We'll be in clear air soon as we near the coast."

Falk kept a firm grip as he stared out the window at the swirling mass of snow. Being taken to the airstrip would allow him to fly his copter to the lighthouse and, hopefully, get him there before dark.

Chapter 71

Inside the lighthouse, activity was reaching a feverish pitch. The main door was secured shut and the dining table pushed against it. Commander Harris and Tanner sealed the scientific documents in a cylindrical metal tube, having agreed that the tube would remain in their collective charge at all times. Neither trusted the other out of his sight.

Koski and Dr. Clayton secured the cellar room, making sure the movable section of the wall was closed. Kevin suggested they *not* brace it, instead making sure the door could be opened quickly from the inside in case they had to use the tunnel as an emergency exit.

The time had come and gone for the code exchange. By now the Royal Navy should have been checking the occupants. Tanner was even more acerbic than usual. "This would never have happened if we'd had the United States Navy on patrol, I can assure you."

"I suppose they would have been as well prepared as they were in Yemen when two Arabs in a rubber boat blew up a US Navy vessel in port." Commander Harris' voice dripped with sarcasm as he stuffed a blanket onto the window frame of a staircase window, aware darkness would soon envelope them. Winter, in the north of Scotland had no twilight. He stopped and looked intolerantly at Tanner. "I asked that weapons be stored in the lighthouse, and was assured that there would be no need. Security agents would take care of us. Well, to date we've had two killed. That we know of. One has secretly returned to the mainland, and one is lost out there in the company of an old Scotsman about whom we know virtually nothing except that, despite your agents, he sneaked in here and has been living beneath our feet without our knowledge."

Koski interrupted before the argument developed into a yelling match. There simply wasn't time for this. "Listen up. We weren't able to do the code exchange, and by my best reckoning, the Navy should have been here by now. We must assume that for some reason, they're delayed or perhaps something drastic has caused a change of plans." She paused. "Unless they were given an order to stand down."

"You said communications were burnt out," Dr. Jenner said.

"They are."

"Someone could have sent a message *before* they were burnt up," Ms. Spencer offered as she sat on the bottom step of the staircase.

"The radio room has been guarded twenty-four hours, night and day, ever since we moved in. No unauthorized person entered," Koski growled in reply.

"I wouldn't be so sure," Professor Teesdale ventured. "Odd things have been happening ever since we came here and began our meeting." The professor glanced at the others as if seeking reassurance.

"If no one was able to get into the radio room and send a false message, then why hasn't the Navy shown up?" Tanner asked.

"I don't know, Mr. Tanner," Koski replied. "What I do know is that when the code implemented, it was agreed that the only communication between us would be the coded exchange. I couldn't simply yell, 'Help'!" Glancing out a half-secured window, she saw it was already dark.

Dr. Clayton stated for everyone, "Then somebody must have given the order to return to base."

"It would have had to originate in the Admiralty itself," the commander huffed.

"At this moment, suppositions are useless. We need to proceed with what we know," Koski said with finality. "The Navy isn't coming. We're on our own."

The Solar Triangle

Chapter 72

When the Coast Guard helicopter finally broke through the clouds, they were passing over Oban. The sky below the thick cloud cover was clear. Fifteen minutes later, the pilot swung his aircraft into position over the small airstrip and lowered softly. Falk could see Constable Slat holding onto his helmet amidst the down draft, his black raincoat flapping like the wings of a raven.

In few moment later, Falk was standing beside Slat and the two were watching the Coast Guard helicopter lift off. "If it wasn't for those guys, I'd still be in a snowstorm telling stories to a pub owner in Clatch."

"Clatch?" Slat looked puzzled.

"Remind me to tell you about it some time." Falk looked sideways at Slat, as if thinking.

"I had a call at the station from Mr. Tom Stewart," Slat volunteered. "He said to tell you the Navy is on its way back to Holy Loch. The orders came from 'Flag' at the Admiralty. At the moment, no one there knows who the 'Flag' issuing the orders actually was."

Falk immediately thought of Koski and the others in the lighthouse. Did that mean that Special Forces had already moved in to protect them?

Constable Slat continued. "I searched the office and old hangar here at the airstrip. The mechanic cleared out, but I found this." He handed Falk a paper bag.

Falk opened the bag and removed a broken slat of wood. Stencilled on one side were stenciled four letters in Cyrillic. "What is it?"

"I'm not sure. I was searching through an assortment of rubbish in the old hangar, and when I kicked an empty box out of my way, I saw that sticking up from the earthen floor. The SAS team had been through earlier and hadn't noticed anything amiss. I was just double-checking. I'd intended to check the place out when I was up here the other day, talking to your mechanic, but a call came through on my cell and I had to return to the office. What do you think it is?"

"The one thing we know for certain is that it's Russian." Both men stared at each other for a moment. "Damn! Those guys we lost at the ferry! They could have hidden out in the old hangar and picked up arms and ammo. If so, they could be on their way to take out the lighthouse."

Slat looked shocked. "'Take out the lighthouse'? Why?"

"Never mind. I've got to get over to the island right away." Falk ran toward the hangar that held his copter, Slat puffing along beside him. First, suspected terrorists slip past the SAS at the ferry, then the Navy gets orders to return to port from a source the Admiralty can't positively identify. It had all begun to fall into place.

The door on the newer hanger was still locked with the sturdy padlock. Falk turned to the constable. "Did you notice any keys in the office when you were checking it out? I've got to get in there now, and I don't want to use a gun. It might damage the aircraft."

"Not that I recall."

"Then we'll have to break in. Come on, let's see what we can find." As they headed together back to the old hangar, darkness fell, and the first large drops of rain began pelting them from an increasingly sullen sky. Falk immediately knew he would would be flying in the face of danger when he flew to the island. He would have to perform a risky night landing in the rain on rocky and treacherous terrain.

Slat switched on his flashlight as soon as they entered the gloomy hangar. "Over there!" he yelled, pointing the beam across the interior to the far wall. "I recall seeing a couple of old steel rebar rods. We can pry the padlock off with one of those." They took one each and jogged back to the helicopter hangar in the darkness and rain. Slat was right. The bars snapped the hasp off the door without problem.

"First time I've ever had help from the law breaking and entering, Slat."

"Aye, and hopefully the last." Together they slid the

heavy door aside and entered. "Over here." Again, Slat, flashlight in hand, walked directly up to a bank of light switches and began throwing on each. Bright overhead lamps thudded on bathing the inside of the hangar in brilliant white light. In the center of the hangar was Falk's helicopter, its neon orange and yellow radial blazing brightly.

Falk walked around the aircraft and began a pre-flight check, paying special attention to the powerful spotlight slung beneath the nose. He was going to need every lumen when he made his final approach to Flangenan Island. Satisfied with the outside check, he swung open the door and climbed into the pilot's seat. He checked the control panel, then ran his hands lightly over the flight controls. The aircraft, as promised, had been well cared for in his absence.

"With your help, Constable, we can push this beauty out and get her warmed up." Working together, they had the helicopter outside in a matter of minutes.

"What's the chance of my going with you out to the lighthouse?" Slat asked. "I might come in handy."

Falk thought for a moment. "I could use someone to stay with the copter after we land. You sure you want to go? This is as dangerous a mission as any I've seen."

Slat's heart jumped. He was going to see action. There was still a chance he would have a story to tell his grandchildren one day. "Aye, I'm sure."

"Then climb in and put on the earphones hanging beside the passenger seat." As he spoke, Falk took his position at the controls and fired up the engine. The blades began their slow rotation, whining and spinning faster by the second until they swished through the air with their own peculiar and somewhat frightening thumping sound. Slat had secured himself in with his seatbelt and was adjusting his headset when Falk's voice crackled through to him. "Can you read me?"

Slat turned toward Falk and gave a thumbs up.

"On the back of one of the earphones, you'll find a microphone. Swing it into position, then you can talk."

"How's that?" Slat asked as he adjusted the microphone.

"Loud and clear. Now, sit back and try to relax. Here we go."

It was the first time Slat had ever been in a helicopter and at the combination of shuddering and separating from the ground made him feel elated. The rush of air and the upward and horizontal movement as they sped across the airstrip, rain slashing across the Perspex bubble surrounding them, was fantastic. The machine quickly gained altitude, bucking the wind gusts from the Atlantic, as Falk set course for Flangenan.

"Are you armed, Constable Slat?"

"No, sir. Against regulations."

"Have you been trained in the use of firearms?"

"Aye. I served in the army back when we all had to do our time. I've done a wee bit of hunting on the moors since. I know enough to keep out of trouble."

"Good. Reach beneath your seat. You'll find a metal box. Slide it out."

Slat did so. Placing the box on his knees, he opened the lid.

"That's a nine millimeter Smith and Wesson six-six-nine. It has a twelve round capacity. Any problems?" Falk asked.

"None what-so-ever," an even more excited constable replied, weighing the weapon in one hand.

"Fine. The safety's on, but it's cocked and loaded. Check the location of the safety and remember it. You might have to find it in the dark."

Falk fingered the weapon he'd taken from Abu Scha and placed in his jacket pocket. Quickly, he removed the automatic and replaced it in a zippered outside pocket of his flight suit, then, squinting ahead into the blackness of the rainy night, expertly piloted the small aircraft forward. If everything went well, they would arrive over their destination in a matter of minutes.

Chapter 73

Swale and Jock were eating shared rations with their captors beneath a plastic ground sheet as the rain, now steady, poured into the shallow trench they shared with two of the Special Service men. Jock leaned back against the muddy wall. "If I dinna get a real drink soon, I'll die. A mon needs a wee dram every day to stay alive."

Swale smiled. "You had enough to drink in that cellar you were living in to last the rest of your life."

"Aye, if I die in the next minute, and I dinna intend to do that."

Swale asked one of the soldiers what the plan was now that communications were out. Were they sitting and waiting for back up? If their headquarters attempted to make contact and couldn't get through, what would happen next? The man closest to him explained that when a six-man team is dropped on a target, they are a self-contained unit, expected to complete their objective and make their way back to a prearranged location. In this case, since the objective was to protect a lighthouse on a small island, when the meetings were over, the Navy would remove the scientists and the Special Service men would remain hidden unless needed. Either way, they would return with the scientists and Navy. If there was a need to protect the meeting scientists and staff, their unit was to reveal themselves and take care of the problem.

"So we're prisoners until the Navy gets back?"

"That's what the Sarge said." The soldier adjusted his night vision binoculars and scanned the lighthouse. He'd said all he was going to.

"Listen," Swale said. The two soldiers heard it also: the unmistakable sound of a low flying helicopter.

"Two o'clock," the soldier with the night vision binoculars called, then winced as a stab of brilliant white light cut through the rain and began moving jerkily from side to side. The glare finally resolved into a fixed downward shaft of light as the helicopter swung around the outer edge of the island, moving ever nearer to the lighthouse as it lowered closer to the rocky ground. "That crazy bastard is going to try and land in this weather at night."

No one spoke further. They watched as the source searchlight slowly lowered; the helicopter itself could not be seen, obliterated by the swirling rain. Swale heard the metallic rasp of automatic weapons being cocked, and the sergeant's voice ordering, "Hold your fire! Wait for my whistle. Let the silly bugger land or crash."

Swale recalled Falk saying he'd be back around dusk. Could this be him? Suddenly, the silhouette of a copter congealed from within the bleakness, and a figure could be seen in the helicopter's bubble for a split second.

"Sergeant," offered Agent Swale. "I believe the pilot of that helicopter is the security agent in charge of the scientists' detail: Agent Joseph Falk."

"Says who?"

"He's due back here tonight. He's been on the mainland and he could be carrying news about the communications breakdown."

"If he flies that fucking copter any closer to the lighthouse in this weather and tries to land, he'll plough into the ground and become an ex-security agent."

Everyone watched as the the helicopter circled, roaring louder and louder, seeking a spot that would afford a safe landing.

The Solar Triangle

Chapter 74

Koski and Tanner crowded close together, straining to see out of the only window they'd not yet stuffed with blankets and reinforced shut.

"That's him. That's Joe! He's back!" Koski loudly announced to all who heard her.

"Maybe. But I can't see how he's going to land in this weather in the dark. It's complete madness," Tanner muttered.

The Solar Triangle

Chapter 75

McLean and his men made their landing just before the rain started. They advanced under the cover of darkness in the direction of the lighthouse, each man having covered his boots with a pair of thick woollen socks to lessen the chance of being heard. McLean and his men stopped as one when they heard the thumps of a helicopter rotor above. He suspected the aircraft was looking for them, and when the searchlight appeared felt certain. "Stay still. Let it circle and wait for it to land. Once on the ground, we'll take it out."

"If he can land it in this rain and wind," one of the men said.

"It's not military," McLean replied. "You can tell by the engine sound. It could be the small civilian copter from the airstrip."

Together they watched in silence as the aircraft made an attempt at a landing, a gust of wind tossing it perilously close to the lighthouse. The pilot obviously wrestling with the controls to avoid being flung against the cylindrical structure. Nonetheless, McLean signalled his men to disperse, and they vanished like a stream of cockroaches under light.

The Solar Triangle

Chapter 76

When the wind calmed for a few seconds, Falk made his decision. It had to be now.

He pointed the small helicopter at the ground and it slid down its own beam of light, landing on the wooden pier that jutted out to sea. Falk knew as the aircraft set down that he'd made a wise choice. The day he and Zas had come ashore, he'd noticed how sturdy and well-constructed the pier looked.

As the copter settled firmly in place, its rotors winding down, Falk gave last minute instructions to Slat. "At the end of the pier you'll find coils of rope. Secure the copter, tie down the front and back, and tie a couple of hitches to the skids. Then stay here on the pier."

Falk removed his earphones, opened the door, slid out, and as he quickly ran along the pier towards the front door of the lighthouse, the door opened to him.

Koski, the first out of the lighthouse door, flung her arms around his neck, and for a few seconds they remained entwined. "Thank God, you made it," she gasped.

Falk moved the two of them inside, gave her a kiss, shut the door and slid the bolts across. "Are you okay?"

"I'm fine. But we have big problems, Joe."

The Solar Triangle

Chapter 77

McLean's second-in-command had remained next to him. "We can move down there," he whispered, "and take that copter out with no problem." But a new thought had entered McLean's devious mind.

He checked his watch. Their attack was due to start in fifteen minutes. He'd let the helicopter remain where it was. If, after they had the documents and killed all the scientists and their staff, the helicopter from Abu Scha didn't make it, or crashed on landing, he would force the pilot of the private copter to fly him out, after he'd made sure the rest of his men and the informer would never leave the island.

"Leave it where it is," McLean whispered back. "I want three rocket propelled grenades directed at the lighthouse, at least one RPG to blast open the front door. Then we move in as planned."

The Solar Triangle

Chapter 78

While Falk learned what had happened inside the light-house, the sergeant of the Special Forces Team turned and acknowledged one of his scouts who'd silently appeared in the shallow trench. "We've got company, boss," the scout reported. "I sighted a group proceeding toward the lighthouse at ten o'clock from this position, about 700 yards down slope."

Adjusting his night vision binoculars, the NCO parsed the area. He thought he saw a slight movement, but only fleetingly. "If they're there, they're good. Did you get a count?"

"No, but I'd guess four to six."

"Right. Escort our two 'guests' here back to the pipe. Stay with them and don't let them out of your sight." To Swale and Jock huddled near him in the trench, he stated, "Try anything and you'll be shot. Understand?" Both men nodded dismally, the rain increasing until it ran in streams off their heads and shoulders.

The sergeant then snapped orders for the others to remain alert and await his signal: three blasts on his whistle. Then move in on the unknown invaders.

The hand signal orders were barely finished when the stone sides of the lighthouse before them were abruptly engulfed in a ball of fire. changing the squad leader's plans. "Bloody hell! Whoever it is down there just blew the fucking door of the lighthouse off its hinges!"

Chapter 79

Constable Slat almost fell off the pier when the RPG went off. He reacted, ducking reflexively against the side of the helicopter. Orange-red flashes followed by the sputtering cough of automatic gunfire appeared from around the lighthouse, announcing clearly that it was under concentrated fire. Keeping low, Slat opened the passenger door, reached in and retrieved his "Bobby" helmet, then, feeling more properly dressed, scuttled along the pier toward the lighthouse with his newly acquired 9 mm held at ready. Anyone seeing him, raincoat flapping in the wind, holding the top of his helmet with one hand, would have wondered what in hell a country copper was doing in such a situation. In his mind, Constable Slat was charging the beaches at Normandy.

The Solar Triangle

Chapter 80

Luckily, when the front door blew apart there was no one in the immediate vicinity to be injured. Falk had directed everyone as far from the front door as possible, but first, he'd had them haul in several heavy wood meeting room tables and place them on a side in front of it as a barricade. He'd had several more placed on their side on the other side of the room as a makeshift blast wall. With the onset of this attack, he knew a team of SAS men prepositioned in the area would come running on the double. All they had to do inside the lighthouse was keep their heads down and wait.

One occupant of the besieged lighthouse also knew it would only be a matter of minutes before being spirited away from the island. Assignment completed, years of research by three of the top scientists in the world and the results of three days collating information, and the awesome power of solar energy were complete. But, as the traitor mused, and had been decided in Syria, it could soon be harnessed for warfare and the obliteration of all Syria's enemies.

The Solar Triangle

Chapter 81

When Tom Stewart learned that the Royal Navy was heading back to base at Holy Loch, he knew Koski and Falk were in even more danger. *Cerberus,* as usual, through discrete methods unavailable to others, had always been fully aware of the pre-arranged signals between the lighthouse and the Royal Navy. Immediately after being given the news about the Royal Navy turning back, Stewart was talking directly with the British Admiralty, Flag Signals office, Whitehall, London, where he was assured that, yes, a message had been sent, relieving HMS Exeter and Ajax from security patrol in the Outer Hebrides and reordering their return to base. When asked on whose orders the message had been transmitted, he was told to stand by.

Drumming his fingers on his desk in anxious anticipation, he felt he knew already, and the outcome of the entire operation could well involve everyone on the island losing their life, despite the small force of Special Service troops he had arranged in place. Abu Scha might be dead, but the man's plan was still in action.

The computer printer began clacking across the room, breaking Stewart's train of thought. The message was from the Admiralty to a cover name, The United States Department of Naval Logistics, being used by *Cerberus* for the Secret meetings.

> *GO TO SECURE PHONE RED687. DO NOT USE ANY OTHER MEANS FOR FURTHER DISCUSSION ON THIS SUBJECT. OUT.*

Stewart picked up the handle of the secure phone kept in a desk drawer for just this purpose and tapped in the sixteen digit authentication code kept only in his mind.

Chapter 82

"Go to the back of the room. Stay away from windows." Falk's voice carried sharply above the din, and everyone quickly obeyed. "There's an allied Special Service team on the island. At this very moment, they'll be moving in on whoever's out there trying to break into the lighthouse."

Falk turned to Koski, keeping his voice low. "What happened to the code exchange? Where's the Navy?" Two windows had blown out and a hail of automatic fire outside could be heard, some of the bullets raking the the interior walls of the lighthouse.

"Long story, Joe," Koski replied, "but essentially we're on our own."

Falk scanned the room. Tanner and the commander were huddling together behind one of the large tables they'd turned on its side, the metal tube between them on the floor.

Falk turned to Koski, about to ask what was lying on the floor, but she spoke before he had a chance. "The entire results of the meetings are in that tube and neither of them wants it out of their sight." The sound of automatic gunfire increased.

"If whoever's attacking gets a solid bead on one of those

two blasted out window frames, we'll be blown to hell." Tanner's words had a hard edge to them, emphasizing their increasingly fragile situation.

"Doctor Clayton and Koski secured the cellar. We could all go down there and wait it out," Courtney Spencer suggested.

"I told you, it's not safe down there, we don't know..." Koski began.

"There's a damn big hole now where the front door was," the commander rasped. "We don't know who's outside. We could all be killed trying to make our way down there."

"Everyone wait here," Falk commanded. "I'll check outside." Creeping from behind the barricade of furniture, he cautiously peered out into the room. Smoke layered the air and hung close to the floor. Crouching, he made his way to the shattered up-sided tables they had pressed against the door. The tables had been pushed several feet to the side, creating a slot between the table top and wall. Rounding the corner of the table, he could see outside yellow flashes of flame against the blackness from bursts of automatic weapons. Falk held his gun at ready, although it would be of little use against the weaponry he was hearing, when suddenly a black figure spun through the door and flattened itself against an inside wall. Falk was about to fire at the intruder when he recognized the unique shape of Constable Slat's high crowned helmet.

"Slat! Over here!" The constable saw Falk and gave a wave of recognition. "Stay there, I'll coming around."

Seconds later, he crouched beside Slat who was the first to speak. "The firefight has swung away from the lighthouse. There's a group up on the slope." He pointed into the darkness. "I was pinned down, when the shrapnel and pieces of the lighthouse from that last RPG flew about. I feared I wouldn't survive another, so I decided to get inside while I could."

"Special Service team," Falk said quickly. "The group on the slope. They made a HAHO drop several hours ago and have been dug in waiting in case they were needed."

"At least somebody was thinking ahead," Slat muttered.

"Now it's time for more thinking. I have a roomful of people back there." Falk pointed up the second barricade of tables at the far end of the room. "I've got to get them to a place of safety until the Navy arrives."

"When will that be?"

"Soon, I hope." Falk crossed the area and pulled back the carpet to reveal the trapdoor.

"What's that?"

"That, Constable, is where our old Scottish friend, Jock, the old man who used to live here, Jock, was hiding out when I found him. He damn near killed me."

"Aye, well, old Jock was known to have a short temper shortened further by drink."

"Given our present situation, I'm going to split the group: three in the cellar and three in the radio room. Keep an eye on this doorway while I sort them out." Just before he turned to leave, Falk grinned. "Enough adventure for you, Slat?"

"Aye, sure enough. Next time I'll be more careful what I wish for," said the old constable, squinting into the darkness where the front door had been.

It had stopped raining and the gunfire was down to sporadic bursts. Adding to the freezing cold, his thick regulation police shirt was damp with sweat.

Chapter 83

A camouflaged soldier ushered Swale and Jock to the pipe, ordered them into the first few feet and told them to sit with their backs against the curved wall of the cold iron pipe.

"Don't move. You'll live or die by following orders. Understand?" the soldier asked.

Swale and Jock nodded in unison, watching as the soldier faded from the entrance. Neither doubted his word, but Jock spoke for them both: "If that wee soldier thinks I'm going to sit here on my arse waiting for him, he's wrong." He immediately clarified, adding, "I need a drink and know where to find one."

Without answering, Swale joined Jock standing in the middle of the pipe. Freed from their restraints by their captors in case Swale and Jock, too, became ensnared in the fire fight, Swale answered, "Come on, then," and together they moved down the pipe toward the secret door.

Once, when he was a kid, Swale had played hide and seek in the cellar of an old fruit market in London. He and his friends loved it down there among the fruit crates. He could never forget the various smells of the ripe oranges, plums, cherries, currants, red and black grapes and nectarines. Stacks of crates, some full, others empty, stood in long orderly rows. The only illumination was from a single 40-watt light bulb suspended from a low arched ceiling. The whitewashed brick walls added a sense of eeriness to the huge cellar, heightening the excitement the kids felt when they trespassed on the property, for it was, after all, a forbidden playground. As Swale stumbled along the pipe in the dark, he recalled his nervous excitement of so long ago. This time, however, the seekers would not tag him and laugh shrilly with delight. This time, they would kill him.

Chapter 84

"I'll take those plans." Doctor Jacob Jenner's voice was strained but firm as he indicated the metal tube on the floor between Tanner and the commander. "It's obvious neither of you trust the other, so I think it's better if one of us scientists be the guardian." Jenner finished as Falk appeared from behind the barricade.

Damn it, Falk thought, *will they never stop arguing? They're worse than kids.* "No, *I'll* take it," he said stooping and picking up the metal tube. "Listen to me now. There are two areas of the lighthouse that currently offer the best security." Falk pointed at Jack Tanner. "Mr. Tanner, Professor Teesdale, and Doctor Clayton, down into the cellar. Commander, you, Doctor Jenner and Ms. Spencer go with Agent Koski to the radio room."

"You said Special Forces were out there," Courtney Spencer flared.

"And they are. And I hope they've have taken care of whoever was trying to get in for these." Falk tapped the metal tube. "But until I'm absolutely positive we're safe, we split into two groups and retreat to the two safest places available. Now, let's move."

The Solar Triangle

Chapter 85

When bullets from the hidden Special Service team hit and killed two of McLean's team, he didn't panic. He simply faded into the blackness, carrying two RPGs and his AK47, moving ever closer to the lighthouse. His remaining men returned fire, trying to defend their leaders and themselves against a cunning adversary that seemed to have appeared from nowhere.

McLean knew that Abu Scha's helicopter was due at any time. The worst of the storm had all but passed, and the wind was dying—both good signs. He'd have to gamble that whoever was engaging his men wouldn't shoot his copter down when it appeared. It was a chance he had to take. On the other hand, was it?

McLean had been a street fighter since the age of eleven. The monotonous rows of back-to-back brick houses, narrow alleys, and streets of Bogside in Belfast had been his training ground. His mentors were the meanest and hardest of the IRA.

He could see the gaping hole where the lighthouse door had once been. He would have been inside by now if it hadn't been for the surprise attack. A sense born of harsh experience signalled him from within. *Special Service bastards. Fucking SAS!* For a moment, the hatred he'd harbored since he was a child welled, but quickly, he forced himself to be calm. If the SAS were on the island, it meant his plan was no longer a secret. Instead of appearing and disappearing like ghosts, they'd walked into an ambush.

McLean had to make a decision. Scha's helicopter hadn't appeared. Still, he could make his way back to the Zodiac and quietly push out to sea, lose himself amid the waves, and make a landing on an empty shore miles away. But then what? He'd have to spend the rest of his life looking over his shoulder with both the Syrians and the SAS after him. He shrugged deeper into his wet coat. On the other hand, Scha's helicopter might have been delayed by the storm. When it came, he could locate his contact, pick up the plans, eliminate the contact, deliver the package to Scha and collect a million dollars. And if Scha's copter didn't materialize at all, he still had his backup plan involving the helicopter at the pier. He decided to wait.

Chapter 86

Stewart hung up the secure phone in disbelief. The report he'd been given fortified the fact that the person in the lighthouse, the informer, had been well briefed. According to the message, Flag Communications in London had gone through the tapes from the recording computers at an ultra-secret location near Jodel Bank's Astro Communications in England, a location that routinely monitored and recorded every word and sound transmitted by satellite, computer e-mails, radio transmissions, and phone conversations worldwide. What had once been but a dream was today an actuality in the British world of electronic eavesdropping. Flag had traced the signal sent to the HMS Ajax and Exeter, verifying it was, in fact, transmitted from an airstrip on the Island of Tiree.

Unbeknown to Stewart, the mechanic had made the transmission, using secret frequencies and procedures supplied to Abu Scha's terrorist organization by an unknown source privy to the security arrangements at the international meeting in the lighthouse.

Stewart smiled. By involving Falk and Koski in the meeting, he had placed them in exactly the right place at the right time. The last piece of information he had received from London proved without a doubt that the English did indeed have a top secret piece of intelligence-gathering hardware, something often spoken of as a far distant possibility in intelligence circles around the world. The British Signal Interceptor, in the twenty-first century, was as important as their wartime wonder of the early forties, radar. Whoever had been able to get hold of the frequencies and sell them to Abu Scha could surely be able to obtain other pieces of the puzzle. And that person was in the lighthouse with nowhere to run. Falk must find the unknown informant at all costs, along with the SOLAR/HAARP agreements.

Chapter 87

Jock squeezed into the cellar and went straight for his supply of Scotch. It was pitch black, and Swale could hear the rattling of bottles, followed by the unmistakable squeak of a cork being removed, then the steady glug, glug of a tipped bottle held to the lips.

"Light a lamp, man. I can't see a damn thing in here," Swale complained.

Three glugs later before Jock answered. "Hold your horses. I canna find the matches."

"Didn't have a problem finding the booze though, did you?"

"Ah, here they are." Swale heard the rattle of a match box, then saw by a sudden flare as Jock touched the match to the wick, followed by a constant glow as Jock replaced the glass chimney onto lamp. A column of black smoke snaked toward the ceiling, lessening as the flame established itself. "There ye are, laddie, all the comforts of home," he said, rummaging in a cardboard box to present a can of baked beans. "Would ye join me in a bite to eat?"

Before Swale could answer, they heard the sound of the trapdoor above being opened. Jock reached to where he usually kept his revolver. "Ach. That damned Yank took it with him."

Falk came down the ladder, the document case slung on his shoulder.

"That very Yank," confirmed Jock.

When Falk recognized Swale and the Scot, he called up to the others. "Don't come down, yet; I need to make more room down here." Turning to Swale, he asked, "What the hell happened to you two?" as he started began unscrewing the cap on the document tube.

Pointing at Jock, Swale replied, "We became guests of a military squad until ol' Jock here decided he needed some refreshment, so we're back where we started."

Jock was busy cutting the top off the can of beans with an old fashioned can opener.

"Special Service guys," Falk said. "They could be here any moment." He glanced toward the brick door.

"Things were pretty busy when we last saw them," Swale reported. Jock, spooning heaps of beans into his mouth, some of them falling into his beard, didn't seem to miss a word.

"I'm putting three members of the meeting down here for safety," Falk said, as he slid the papers out of the tube and looked around the room. "I need a safe place to stash these," he declared softly.

Swale pointed to the filthy, unmade bunk. "Over there. Under the straw mattress on the bunk. I doubt anyone will go near that."

Jock glared, but continued to spoon in beans between swigs of whisky.

Falk slid all the papers under the disgustingly dirty paillasse. Swale was right. No one would want to touch the squalid bed. "We have to find a way to signal for help. The Navy should have been here long ago."

Jock took a particularly long swig. "Ye seem to forget where ye are. This is a lighthouse, mon. This is what these places were built for. We can send a light signal."

Falk and Swale exchanged glances. It made sense.

"I've enough oil stored away. We can pile up some furniture and use these two oil burners to get it started" The surly Scott jabbed a grimy finger at the table lamps. "While ye get your people down here, we'll go up to the lantern room an' I'll show you what an old fashioned lighthouse keeper can do with those old reflecting lenses."

"Right," Falk replied. "I'll go with Jock. You stay, Swale. And remember: There's an informer in our midst." Falk glanced once again around the room. "And don't let anyone get near those papers. Okay, Jock, we'll leave one lamp and take the other." He picked up the unlit lamp and shook it. "Needs topping up; where's the oil?"

Jock rummaged in the small adjoining room in which he'd hidden when Falk had first found him. It seemed like a month ago, but was really, just a few days. He came out carrying a five gallon drum. "Lead on, McDuff. Lead on."

Falk, the now empty tube slung over one shoulder and carrying the lit oil lamp in one hand, climbed up the ladder, then reached down, grabbed the oil drum from Jock and hauled it up.

Chapter 88

Mr. Tanner, Professor Teesdale, and Dr. Clayton were crouching against the wall under Slat's watchful eye. "Okay, Constable, Mr. Swale below will take care of them." Falk watched as they descended into the cellar, then replaced the trapdoor and carpet, and headed up the stairs to the radio room, Jock and Slat in tow.

Koski looked up as the door to the radio room opened, and Falk said, "We're going to start a fire in the lantern room. Jock says we can send out a light signal that will be seen for miles. We need anything on this floor that will burn. Tables chairs; if it'll burn, we need it." Jock was already heading high up the last rungs into the lens room, carrying the oil drum under one massive arm.

"Where did he come from?" Koski asked upon seeing the old Scot again.

"He made it back. I found him and Swale in the cellar. I left Swale in charge of Tanner, Clayton, and the Professor. This gentleman is Constable Slat, the lone constable of Oban we talked about a few days ago. He'll help you collect anything that will burn and pass it up to us."

In the darkness of the lighthouse room, Jock had stumbled across the body of Zas. After receiving the oil lamp from Falk, he took the blanket off of the corpse. "I'm nah a heathen, but we need this to get the grime off the lenses." He ripped the blanket into hand size pieces. "We'll need all hands to get them clean, laddie, tell them below to get up here now."

Within minutes, Koski, the commander, Doctor Jenner, Cortney Spencer and Constable Slat were rubbing away the dirt of ages from the once pristine glass, now cracked, and in places, chipped and brown-spotted. "I've polished this lens hundreds of times over the years. It will be grand to see the prisms come back to life, if even for a wee short time"

The lens, mounted in bronze fittings, was eight feet in diameter and fifteen feet high. Falk noticed the workmanship for the first time and commented on it.

"Aye, she's a Fresnal lens from a French furnace in St. Gobain. One thousand twenty-four separate prisms. When she was first installed, the five ton light was so delicately balanced on heavy bronze rollers that my father could rotate the lens with his little finger." As Jock spoke and polished, pieces of wood and furniture continued being hauled up, broken into kindling and placed into the old original oil containers.

Finally, Jock announced the pile as high enough to light, but ordered them to continue fetching anything that would burn; once lit, they would have to keep the fire as bright as possible.

Falk grunted as he heaved another bundle of broken furniture pieces into place on the pile.

"I'll scout around and find some more," Slat said.

"No, you stay with Koski and keep the fire going. Once I see the fire is under control, I'll take a crew with me to break up the barricade across the room from the entrance and transfer the pieces up here."

"It's time," Jock pronounced proudly. "Pass me the oil." Standing astride the rim above the oil containers, he slid a bottle out of his pocket and took a long draw before carefully replacing his beloved malt back into his pocket.

"Take it easy, old timer. We still need you to operate this contraption."

The Solar Triangle

Chapter 89

McLean caught sight of movement inside the lighthouse. Pressing into the brush, he watched as a lone figure cautiously approached the broken entrance and peered in. The battle was still in progress, although moving away from the lighthouse as McLean's two remaining men attempted a fighting retreat back to the cove, seeking the safety of their Zodiacs in hope of making an escape. The man McLean was watching slid into the building. For a moment he toyed with the idea of firing an RPG grenade into the lighthouse and charging in behind the explosion. His fingers curled in readiness around the trigger of the RPG, but once again, his natural animal cunning took over. Those inside had had time to regroup and make decisions on how to defend the lighthouse. If he entered like a fool, he would die like one.

Despite the darkness, he could see part way into the damaged structure. It appeared as if a wall had been hastily erected just inside the entrance, but between the edge of the lighthouse and new inner wall, he could just make out movement. *What are they doing?* he wondered. Slowly he eased forward, creeping silently closer, one foot at a time, the AK47 slung across his chest in the ready-to-fire position.

He'd released the safety catch long ago and was ready for anything. Approaching the entrance, he lowered himself to the ground and slithered closer using his elbows and toes to move forward. He could hear the murmur of voices and snatches of a conversation. "Constable...take...of them."

Then he heard the clatter of footsteps running up the stairs. To McLean, it sounded as if someone had given orders to take care of someone, then a group had gone up the stairs. Were there guards, ordered to remain on the lower floor while the others went up to reinforce the higher parts of the light-house?

Whatever the case was, Scha's helicopter hadn't come, and he was running out of time. He had to make his move and enter the place, find the informer and plans, then leave with the helicopter pilot. He rose to his feet and began to enter when he heard loud voices. They were not attempting quiet; he could hear every word clearly including the sounds of grunts and the moving of objects being pushed and lifted. Whatever it was they were doing was being carried out fast and efficiently in an organized manner.

McLean slipped inside, his senses tuned for the slightest move from anywhere on the ground floor. Inside the rubble strewn room, he could make out a group of figures across the room smashing up what appeared to have been a hastily erected barrier. He remained still, silent and unmoving until the last piece had been moved up into the lighthouse. Finally, there was silence. The people, finished with their work, had apparently abandoned this floor. When he could no longer see anyone above, he slowly crossed the room, staying close to the wall, every nerve alive and tense. He preceded up the first set of stairs, his eyes fixed on the green painted door ahead. Approaching it, he heard voices and the sounds of activity from behind the closed door.

The Solar Triangle

Chapter 90

Jock started to pour the contents of the five-gallon oil drum they'd hauled up over the pile of combustibles. Emptied, he tossed the container onto the unlit pyre, his eyes ablaze with the excitement of once again awakening his beloved lantern.

"Jock, get on with it. We have to hurry," Falk called out.

"Aye, and I will," he replied, reaching for the lit oil lamp. "Stand away, back against the walls. It'll go off with a roar, and I dinna want any of ye burnt to a crisp."

"No one is going to be burned, but unless you carefully hand me that oil lamp, you will all be shot dead," a voice from against the wall said.

Jock stood, momentarily transfixed, handed the lamp to to the commander, who was standing a few feet from him, aiming a 9 mm automatic directly at Jock.

Jock was by no means the only person in the lantern room shocked at what had happened.

"What the hell is going on, commander?" Falk roared.

"I would like you all to stand single file against the wall," the commander said, indicating the wall opposite the door leading outside with the barrel of his weapon. "And

Falk, kindly place the document tube on the floor and push it toward me. Use your foot and do it slowly."

Falk carried out the order, never taking his eyes off the commander's weapon. "So, you're the informer."

"Afraid so, old boy. I've waited a long time for this." The commander nodded, a sneer distorting his face. He scooped up the document tube with one hand, never taking his eyes off the group against the wall.

"Whatever your plan is, you'll never get away with it."

"Oh, I think I will. The plan is bigger than just me. There are others involved."

McLean, having climbed the rest of the way up the ladder, had been able to hear what was going on. The moment the commander revealed himself, McLean quietly entered the room. No one noticed. They were all still staring in disbelief at the commander.

"I'll soon be going from here to the mainland…"

McLean could not have written a better entrance line. Stepping centerstage, he announced, "And the luck of the Irish is still with me." The commander, at that moment, was as surprised as anyone in the room. "And I'm the man whose going to take you to the mainland. But as a precaution, I need you to tell me the name of the man we're going to meet there."

"Abu Scha," replied the stunned commander. "I didn't

hear the helicopter land."

"There's one waiting outside." McLean looked over the group. "Which one of you flew the copter in here before the shooting?"

"He did." The commander pointed at Falk.

"Fine, now that we have the documents, I only need a hostage to assure that things remain safe and sound." He walked slowly around the room, never taking his eyes off of the two women.

"The man who's going to fly the helicopter is an American agent," the commander offered. "That's his partner, standing next to the tall blonde."

"What does the blonde do?"

"She's one of the government mediators."

McLean moved next to the commander. Seeing Falk's eyes flicker several times towards Koski, McLean concluded, "The American agent has a vested interest in seeing that his partner doesn't get hurt." Nodding at Koski, he continued, "You're now my official hostage. If everyone does as he's told, you'll live."

"I have the documents. Let's go," the commander said, shaking the tube. Suddenly his face changed and the twisted smile faded from his pompous face. "Wait." He shook the tube again.

Unscrewing the cap from the container, the commander

tipped it upside down and shook vigorously. Thrusting his hand inside the tube, he desperately grasped for the documents. His face reddened as he glared at Falk. "What did you do with them?"

Falk tried to look surprised. "I've no idea what you're talking about, Commander."

"Liar! I had everything in here: the plans, the agreement, and every piece of paperwork from the last three days. I risked my life for the damn things."

"And in doing so, Commander, turned traitor to your country."

The commander's face hardened. "My country turned on me, Mr. Falk. I dedicated my life to my country and what good did it do? My home was sold to some dark skinned Arab whose only claim to living in my home, in my country, was he had the money to do so. I had to sell Blaydon Hall, my ancestral home that had been in the family for four hundred years. Owned and cared for by men who, when asked, went off to fight for England no questions asked and served King, Queen, and country and, in most cases, die. I was forced to sell because I couldn't pay the exorbitant inheritance taxes from the measly salary I was paid during all the years of my service. And what's evern worse, no one except me cared. I was of the generation *expected* to die penniless and be quickly forgotten. There are fewer of us every day, and when we are gone, there will be no one to inform the youth what it's like to live in a country that made one proud. A country, small as it is, that was once known worldwide for fair play, law and justice. Look at it now: a melting pot of different nationalities, each distrusting the next. Fights and riots, unrest and unhappiness covered and hidden by drugs and the cacophany they call 'music'. Add to that, politicians hell bent on selling Britain's last vestiges of honor to the EU. Dim witted, dumbed-down, poorly educated kids who have never learned the importance of history and patriotism, but who can reel off reams of words from Rap songs and name every fast food place in their town. Call me a traitor. Perhaps I am. When I deliver the papers, I'll be able to buy back my ancestral home and live my remaining years as I once re-membered English life to be." Taking a deep breath, his voice still quivering from his outburst, he continued. "I'm prepared to kill everyone in this room unless you tell me where the pa-pers are."

Falk, knowing he meant every word, replied, "I hid them in the cellar."

McLean motioned with his AK47. "Lead the way, Mr. Agent and flock, and when we get to the bottom of the stairs, stand once again with your backs to the wall."

It was a dispirited group that filed down from the lens room under the watchful eyes of McLean and the commander. Falk noted that the sound of gunfire outside was fading into the distance, and except for the occasional stutter of an automatic weapon, all was becoming quiet. Had the Special Service team gone after McLean's men? Was it possible that one or two of the men, who had parachuted onto the island to defend the lighthouse, could appear and change the tide of events back in their favor?

On the main level, McLean ordered the commander to go with Falk and hold everyone down there at gunpoint, shooting any who made a wrong move without hesitation.

"Swale, another armed agent, is down there," the commander advised, hesitating to accompany Falk.

"Then you, Mr. Falk, will go alone and tell this agent that if there is any attempt to play hero down there, I will shoot one of my captives. Now move! You have one minute to bring back the papers."

Falk rolled back the scorched carpet, lifted the trapdoor and called down to Swale, explaining their situation as he climbed down into the cellar.

In the room, he moved directly to the bunk and removed the papers, whispering to Swale as he did so. "When I leave, immediately get everyone into the pipe. That guy up there might try anything. Once you hear us take off in my helicopter, go back upstairs and start the fire. Koski is a hostage to guarantee I do everything as instructed. When the rescue party arrives, tell them I've flown to the mainland, and that I think the location is going to be close to the farm where I was taken by Abu Scha. It's near a small village called Clatch."

"Thirty seconds, Falk!" McLean's Irish-Belfast twang grated down to him. "Get back back up here or I'll pop one of these folks."

Falk returned topside with the documents in hand. The commander, as soon as he saw them, grabbed them from Falk and made a fast count. A moment later he signalled to McLain. The documents were all there. McLean, satisfied, backed toward the entrance with Koski at his side. He'd disarmed her in the lantern room and was holding her weapon against her head. "I don't want anyone lighting fires, so for your own safety, I want all of you except my hostage and her compatriot in the cellar. Now." One by one, they obeyed.

"Shouldn't we secure the trapdoor?" asked the commander after the last one had left the room.

"Keep these two covered," ordered McLean, sliding the RPG from his shoulder, loading one of the two remaining grenades, calmly firing it into the cellar and closing the trapdoor. There was a loud thump and the floor beneath them lifted several inches then settled in a cloud of dust.

McLean ordered Koski and Falk to remove the table blocking the lighthouse entrance and directed the three out the shattered, gaping doorway. Twenty feet away from the entrance, he turned, reloaded and aimed the last grenade at the inside stairway leading up to the lantern room. The grenade hissed across the short distance and slammed into the stairs with a roar. The blast took out the stairs and a part of the upper wall, leaving the second floor communication room hanging open thirty feet above the main floor.

It was still dark when McLean and the commander hustled Falk and Koski down to the pier. The commander, intent on getting away from the island, completely forgot about the outside stairway. McLean, having approached and exited the lighthouse from the front, never knew it existed..

After releasing the tie-downs, Falk sat at the controls, McLean next to him, Koski and the commander in small pulldown back seats. In the co-pilot's seat, McLean rammed the document tube between his knees.

Falk wound up the engine in preparation for take off. Watching the engine heat gauges for the correct temperature seemed to take forever to Falk. Once the needle hit the required mark, his eyes flicked across the remaining dials, and he noticed he was low on gas. If they ran into a storm or a strong head wind, they might have to make a forced landing.

"Get this thing airborne; I have a rendezvous to make," McLean's harsh voice crackled through the earphones. Falk was about to report they were low on fuel, then changed his mind. The less McLean knew, the better.

The helicopter, carrying a maximum load, lifted clumsily off the pier, then gathered speed, nose down and forward, the usual but peculiar feeling of weightlessness sweeping over them. Falk watched the island fall away beneath them, and made a turn being careful to keep the black iron stairway on the outside back of the white tower from McLean's view.

Falk glanced briefly at the barrel of the automatic being thrust hard by the commander against Koski's side and knew the man would not hesitate to kill her. It bothered him that McLean had seen how much Koski meant to him. *Remain calm and make no sudden moves*, he reminded himself.

The sky was clear. Moonlight shone across the sea like a silver path leading to the mainland. Within minutes they passed over the cliffs of Tiree where he could see one or two lights glimmering in the village. Then they were across the island and over open sea, heading for the mainland.

"Turn north-northeast and continue until we pass over Oban, then east for three minutes," McLean droned. Some minutes later, he continued: "Now go northeast for twelve minutes, maintaining an air speed of ninety knots per hour. At the twelve-minute mark, lower to three hundred feet and decrease air speed. You will circle until I tell you where to set down."

Falk's hunch was right; this placed them directly over

the area near Clatch and the base position from which Abu Scha had been planning to go in search of his connection to Norway. And neither McLean nor the commander apparently had any idea that Abu Scha and his helicopter weren't going to be there waiting.

Chapter 91

Everyone in the pipe on the other side of the brick wall ducked at the thunderous roar of the grenade exploding in the cellar. The ground around the pipe shook and flakes of rust fell from the wet iron interior. Swale had carried out Falk's orders, ushering everyone quickly from cellar to pipe. Dr. Clayton, the last person through the brick door, just made it.

"Everyone okay?" Swale asked the darkness. "Call out your names."

All five answered.

"We may not be able to get back through the cellar and out the trapdoor. In fact, there's a good chance there might not be a cellar. I'll check it out. In the meantime, Constable Slat's in charge. Everyone stay here until I report back."

The small door through the brick wall still worked. As he opened it, acrid smoke poured into the pipe. Swale removed his flashlight from where he'd stored it in his back pocket and snapped it on. The beam cutting through the dust and smoke. He checked the cellar walls which seemed to be in one piece, except for several large chunks of wall that had fallen in from the concussion. There was a crater in the middle of the stone floor where the grenade had made initial impact. The wooden table and chairs were gone, along with the bunk bed. Had they remained in the cellar, they would have been blown to pieces. Skirting the crater, Swale discovered the wooden ladder still firmly affixed to the wall and decided they could make it through the cellar and back up to the lens room.

While everyone began re-assembling in the cellar, Swale attempted to open the trapdoor. It wouldn't budge. When it finally yielded to the the combined efforts of Swale, Jock and Dr. Clayton, the sight, though it was still dark, was overwhelming.

"This entire place could fall down any moment! And the stairs and one wall are almost entirely gone!" Courtney Spencer exclaimed.

"Let's just hope it stays up long enough for us to get to the lantern room and light the fire," Swale urged. "Let's check the outside stairs. C'mon."

Exiting the lighthouse with trepidation, they rounded the lighthouse base and began clattering up the still intact iron staircase in the pre-dawn darkness.

Within minutes, they were inside the lantern room.

"We need to get the fire reflecting off the lenses while it's still dark enough to be noticed, otherwise we'll have wasted our time and effort," Swale muttered. "Light her up, Jock."

The oil lamp was nowhere to be found, so Jock reached in a pocket and pulled out a small box of matches. The first match went out in midair before landing on the stack. The second landed on the wood but nothing happened. The flame flickered momentarily then went out.

Jock cursed in Gaelic, pulled one match part way out of the box and closed the box so the match jutted from it like a small cannon. Then, scraping that match to flame, waited until it began to to singe the box. Slowly he walked to the waiting pyre and laid the box, now beginning to smoke, in the center of the heap and stepped back. WHOOSH! A sheet of flame leapt skyward, the heat causing everyone to move back quickly.

"Bloody hell!" Swale shaded his face against the heat and glare. "Someone should be able to see that in broad daylight."

"Aye, and they will, laddie, ha na fear. The old girl knows how to reflect, I can tell you."

Jock was right. The fire was now growing in strength and the reflectors were gathering every flicker of flame, intensifying the whole into a beam of light a thousand times stronger. Jock took a long swig and passed his tin pocket bottle. "A toast to Flangenan Light, burning bright once again! Now all we need is for sometime to see it. Everyone take a dram for luck. "

The Solar Triangle

Chapter 92

Tanner alone refused to drink. He was thinking of his return to the States and another failed mission. Not his fault, but nonetheless he was part of another failed government project. And he had worked blindly alongside the man who was the cause of his failure: Commander Harris, OBE—the bombastic little limey!

While everyone continued celebrating the light, two Special Service men, a US Navy Seal and the SAS sergeant, entered the room.

The professor saw them first. "I say, seems the beam of light has done its job. We've company already."

Swale looked at the men and shrugged. "Sorry, we couldn't wait for you."

The Solar Triangle

Chapter 93

McLean's voice was tense. "Lower, Falk. Keep her steady." They were hovering over craggy hills of purple heather. It had become light enough for Falk to recognize a few landmarks, one of them the road into Clatch where he'd hitched the ride on the tractor.

Easing the helicopter down slightly and banking, he made a circle of the area below, catching a glimpse of the old farmhouse. He was in an area of swampland and bogs. Not an ideal location to land.

Again, McLean's strained voice crackled over the headset. "Lower, Falk. See where the road rises over the hill, next to that cairn, just east of the small tarn."

Tarn meant lake and Falk saw it at once. The land around it looked increasingly green and soggy as he lowered toward it. He glanced at the gas gauge; it was flickering close to empty. There was only a few more moments of fuel left.

McLean leaned forward to get a better look and noticed the gas gauge. "Take her higher! Now! We have to stay airborne as long as possible. We'll need to lighten our load to conserve fuel." He reached over and placed the barrel of his gun into the commander's ear. "Time for you to leave us, old man."

The commander looked at Falk in despair. Despite the gun, as Falk pulled the controls back to gain height, the commander swung his arm up, grasped McLean's wrist, and pulled hard. McLean, taken by complete surprise at the audacity of such an act, was off guard for a split second, but that was all that was necessary.

Falk kept the nose up and Koski managed a vicious karate chop across the side of McLean's neck, causing him to momentarily black out. Next, she rammed her elbow into the commander's nose, breaking it. He collapsed, groaning and bleeding profusely, totally disoriented.

As McLean re-woke, Koski chopped his wrist, causing his gun to fall to the floor. Falk, seeing his chance, reached across, unsnapped McLean's seat belt, flipped the latch on the side cockpit door, banked sharply to the right, and pushed him out. McLean, still clutching the document tube, never made a sound as he fell, turning over three times before smashing face down into the bog at the edge of the tarn, the document tube still hugged to his chest. Circling, Falk watched the body and tube sink out of sight, the swamp claiming another victim in its ghastly depths.

Koski, averting her eyes from the ugly sight, saw the commander rubbing his bloody nose as he started to regain consciousness. Falk retrieved the automatic from the floor and passed it over his shoulder to Koski, shouting, "If he attempts anything, shoot him!"

"Gladly," Koski answered with a grim glare.

Turning toward Oban, Falk radioed his position and asked for help. Finally out of gas, he would have to make an emergency landing as best he could.

The Solar Triangle

Chapter 94

Less than an hour after the last flicker of light had reflected off the lenses, a Royal Navy pinnace tied up at the jetty. They carried the news that Falk and Koski had been able to overcome their attackers and were safe in Oban where everyone would be meeting later that day. The SAS had taken the commander to an undisclosed location; there were no other details at the moment.

As they walked toward the jetty, Courtney Spencer and Kevin Clayton stopped to look back at the lighthouse where they could see Jock and Swale standing beside the broken front entrance, talking.

"Jock said he was staying at the lighthouse." Courtney shook her head in disbelief. "I would have thought he'd want to get back home after all this."

"It's his home, Courtney. This is where he wants to be," Kevin replied. "Swale suggested that we talk to the powers that be and see if we can arrange for him to move back in on a permanent basis. You know, as a way of saying thanks for all his help."

"I'll second that. Now, about that island you mentioned, the one with lots of sun and very little clothing?"

"You mean the one with the champagne cooling in the sea?"

"That's the place."

They stepped into the Navy pinnace and sat together in the stern.

"It's an ideal place to be in late October, perfect weather."

"Not too many tourists?" Courtney asked.

"None at all. There would be just the two of us, except for the very old couple who look after the place."

"What place is this?"

"Used to belong to a movie actor. I bought the island from him, including the house. Wanna go?"

As the Navy boat readied to move, Swale and Slat scurried on board. Slat waved to Jock as the lines were cast off, and the boat moved slowly away from the jetty.

"Right now, October seems a long time to wait, Kevin," Courtney said.

"There will be lots of meetings between now and then. Did you ever know of a three-government pact where each didn't constantly check up on each other? There'll be meetings in Tel-Aviv, London, and Washington until the project is finished. At the rate governments move, we can make at least three trips to the island for ourselves in between."

Chapter 95

Doctor Jacob Jenner and Professor Victor Teesdale were sitting together deep in conversation, while Jack Tanner sat alone, scowling into the distance.

The debriefing dinner in Oban had proved to be a somber affair. No bagpipes and laughter. Koski and Falk were formally congratulated for their fine work, including thwarting the commander's escape.

Swale was acknowledged for his ability to keep everyone together during the ordeal.

Questions from Courtney Spencer in reference to the outcome of the commander were politely turned aside on the grounds that, due to the gravity of the situation, it was not possible at this time to reveal any details.

"Most likely, they'll lock him in the Bloody Tower and later shoot him," Swale whispered to Dr. Kevin Clayton.

Koski overhearing Swale, grinned and rolled her eyes. "Do they still do that?"

"In England they still do. Sometimes I wish we played by the same rules," Falk replied.

"I feel sorry for him," Courtney said. "That speech he made about all the years of service to his country and his home being sold out from under him."

Tanner, walking by, added, "He's dangerous. People like him have to be removed, the bombastic little bastard."

Chapter 96

"Tom Stewart wants to see us. He's making a stopover at the Tahoe-Truckee airport on his way to Sacramento." Falk hung up the phone and leaned back in his swivel chair. Two months had passed since he and Koski had arrived back home after Operation Solar Triangle.

Koski asked, "Another assignment?"

"He didn't say. Just said to meet him at the airport and he'd buy us dinner. It's a stopover. He has a meeting in Sacramento next morning. He's using a company plane."

Koski crossed the room and sat facing Falk across the desk. She knew what Falk meant when he said "company plane." Stewart was on *Cerberus* business.

"Well, he won't be able to spend much to buy us dinner at the Tahoe-Truckee airport."

Falk laughed. "He told me to make reservations in Truckee."

"Now that's more like it."

The Solar Triangle

Chapter 97

Stewart looked around the dining room of the best, most expensive restaurant in Truckee. "Looks Western."

"Yep, and they serve a great steak. You do eat steak, don't you, Mr. Stewart?" Koski asked teasingly in her most formal voice.

"Yes, I do. And for heaven's sake, Koski, call me Tom." After a brief pause during which all laughed, he added, "Except, of course, in circumstances where protocol is observed."

A waiter came with their drinks. Stewart waited until the man had left before continuing. "As usual, you both did outstanding jobs. Everyone has returned to their respective countries and is back at work, despite the loss of the documents. Our three governments each created a recap of the three day meeting using what their scientist remembered as the primary source. At last word, all was proceeding fine."

After checking to make certain nobody was anywhere near their table, he once again continued. "I wanted to meet with you to give you a little more 'context' as to exactly how important the meeting was. You see, what resulted was a plan for a holographic lens, that projected anywhere above the Earth, could be remotely focused to project down an ultrahigh-energy beam of sulight. Sent to a specially-constructed receiving station, it could be used to generate unlimited pollution-free power, enough to power an entire nation. However, because it is holographic, such a lens could also be directed to pop up anywhere in space to direct a beam at any location. With a little technological tweeking, it could be remotely directed to surgically vaporize anything on Earth or in space. Even rockets and asteroids."

Koski, overawed, sat silent trying to take in the enormity of what they'd been working on and its implications.

Falk finally asked, "And the commander?"

"Yes, well, his case is quite different." Stewart sipped his drink, set it down, and began. "The Arab gentleman who purchased the commander's old home—Blaydon Hall in Sussex—decided the Hall wasn't what he really wanted and put the place up again for sale."

Koski and Falk exchanged puzzled glances.

"You might be wondering what this has with our day-to-day operations at *Cerberus*. Well, for one thing, the fine old home has become part of *Cerberus*. Anyone asking about the new owner will be told a reclusive American Pop artist purchased the estate. A security system *par excellence* has been added to ensure privacy."

"Why does *Cerberus* need a place like that?" Falk asked.

"For one thing, a listening post. We arranged the 'death' of the commander in his wild dash for freedom, and were able to spirit him away under wraps. In short, we made a deal. If he connected us with his man in the Admiralty and helped us tap into his communications, we would give him what he desired so much and would have received from Abu Scha. He agreed. And, in addition, we are getting feedback from his man on how to develop our own signal interceptor system that will enable us to also listen in to any communications around the world."

"You mean you paid the commander and let him off?" Koski asked.

"We paid him, yes, but not to worry. He'll never go free. We know exactly where he is at all times; we made certain of that. Now, let's enjoy the meal. We deserve it."

Afterwards, as they drove back to Reno, Koski said, "Joe, you were right when you said there might be more to our assignment at the lighthouse than we thought. America has, for the first time, a plan for thwarting a missile attack, even a terrorist attack and perhaps even a war. At the same time, Stewart has masterminded a way to steal Britain's Signal Inceptor, locate a mole in the Admiralty we can either turn or use, and the assurance that *Cerberus* will have its own listening post from its secret location at Blydon Hall in Britain."

"And God knows what else," Falk replied.

Chapter 98

It was early April and gardens everywhere were beginning to come to life. A hint of summer rode a breeze blowing softly over the wide green lawns from a distant lake. A solitarly figure stood gazing across the grounds, both hands planted atop a stone balustrade leading to the wide curving steps that had, over the last three hundred years, lead many a fine gathering of crowned heads and members of high society into the gardens to participate in parties, fetes, weddings, and celebrations held at Blaydon Hall.

A smile played the corners of his mouth as he softly quoted a Latin motto carved into the stonework of the fireplace in the great room of the hall. "*Good Fortune is the Comrade of Virtue.*" Commander Harris, now in Cerberus employ, turned, slowly crossed to the French windows of the house and entered his ancestral home.

If you enjoyed *Finding Kate* consider the first book in the Koski and Falk series, *Who's Killing All the Lawyers?*

Lawyers are being murdered by laser-driven arrows. The FBI believes that someone is training Native Americans to take over the US economic system. Joe Falk and Susan Koski are assigned to find the hired killer and The Fox, the real force behind the killings.

GREAT SOUTHWEST BOOK FESTIVAL AWARD
AMAZON KINDLE GENRE BESTSELLER

…the second in the Koski and Falk series, *The Judas List:*

A 700-year-old prayer book, a key and a faded blueprint came to light and begin a search for Nazi Herman Goering's treasure. In modern day Vienna, American agents Koski and Falk must locate the treasure and the Judas List—a compendium of individuals and organizations that financed WWII, and intend to bring about the Fourth Reich.
PACIFIC RIM BOOK FESTIVAL AWARD

…the third book in the Falk and Koski adventure series, *Imminent Danger* by A. G. Hayes.

Jamul, an adored American pop singer, dreams of a grand show of Islamic Jihad power, intending to use a biological weapon to eradicate religious leaders at an Easter service at the Hollywood Bowl. Cerberus agents Joe Falk and Susan Koski must stop the next brutal terrorist attack on American soil.

LOS ANGELES BOOK FESTIVAL AWARD

…the fourth in the multi-award-winning Koski and Falk series, *The Chemical Factor*:

A stolen weapon of mass destruction hidden years ago on board the Queen Mary has remained there undisturbed. Up to now. Agents Falk and Koski are called in to evacuate the ship and somehow locate the bomb. Risking their lives to locate the weapon, they discover that a Girl Scout has strayed from her group during evacuation and is hiding in the ship.

PACIFIC RIM BOOK FESTIVAL AWARD

…the fifth in the multi-award-winning Koski and Falk series and the first in the Kate Keenan Special Assignment series, *Quantum Death*:

Koski and Falk come up against what very well may prove to be their most complex and dangerous case yet: The Quantum Death Machine. Each faces mortal peril, while, at the same time, their smoldering relationship begins to heat up.

AMSTERDAM BOOK FESTIVAL AWARD

…the second in the Kate Keenan Special Assignment series and prequel to *Quantum Death*, *Finding Kate*:

Long-ignored computer genius Kate Keenan has designed a computer program that will put Hollywood and Bollywood out of business. Suddenly everyone wants her…and her program. To stay alive, Kate goes into hiding, barely keeping ahead of a lethal hoard of pursuers with only one thing in mind: *Finding Kate* and possessing or destroying the program.

The Solar Triangle

About the Author

A. G. Hayes studied television writing at UCLA. He has published short fiction for CBS TV and other television production companies. He lives in the Sierra Nevada Foothills and spends his time writing and traveling to nearly every part of the world. He has used personal experiences gained during service with the British intelligence in Eastern Europe and the Middle East to enrich the characters of his protagonist teams. He is the multi-award-winning author of *Who's Killing All the Lawyers* (Savant 2011), *The Judas List* (Savant 2012), *Imminent Danger* (Savant 2013), *The Chemical Factor* (Savant 2015), *Quantum Death* (Savant 2016) and *Finding Kate* (Savant 2016).

The Solar Triangle

352

A. G. Hayes

Chimney Bluffs by David B. Seaburn
The Loons by Sue Dolleris
Light Surfer by David Allan Williams
The Judas List by A. G. Hayes
Path of the Templar - Book 2 of The Jumper Chronicles by W. C. Peever
The Desperate Cycle by Tony Tame
Shutterbug by Buz Sawyer
Blessed are the Peacekeepers by Tom Donnelly/Mike Munger
Purple Haze by George B. Hudson
The Turtle Dances by Daniel S. Janik
The Lazarus Conspiracies by Richard Rose
Imminent Danger by A. G. Hayes
Lullaby Moon by Malia Elliott of Leon & Malia
Volutions edited by Suzanne Langford
In the Eyes of the Son by Hans Brinckmann
The Hanging of Dr. Hanson by Bentley Gates
Written in the Stars - An Anthology edited by Sabrina Favors
Elaine of Corbenic by Tima Z. Newman
Ballerina Birdies by Marina Yamamoto
More, More Time by David Seaburn
Crazy Like Me by Erin Lee
Cleopatra Unconquered by Helen R. Davis
Valedictory by Daniel Scott
The Chemical Factor by A. G. Hayes
Running From the Pack edited by Helen R. Davis
Big Heaven by Charlotte Hebert
All Things Await by Seth Clabough
Captain Riddle's Treasure by GV Rama Rao
Libido Tsunami by Cate Burns
Finding Kate by A. G. Hayes
The Adventures of Purple Head, Buddha Monkey Sticky Feet by Erik Bracht
In the Shadows of My Mind by Andrew Massie
In Search of Somatic Therapy by Setsuko Tsuchiya
Cereus by Z. Roux
Shadow and Light edited by Helen R. Davis

Coming Soon:
A Real Daughter by Lynn McKelvey
StoryTeller by Nicholas Bylotas
Bo Henry at Three Forks by Daniel D. Bradford

http://www.savantbooksandpublications.com

The Solar Triangle